Avasthe

AF668972

Praise for *Avasthe*

'I had read *Avasthe* in a beautiful Malayalam translation decades ago. But looking back now, I feel it is an allegory that suits our times even more than the times when it was written. It is a work central to U.R. Ananthamurthy's oeuvre as it faithfully, if obliquely, reflects his concerns and convictions as a writer and a citizen, making use of the protagonist's paralysis as a metaphor for the democracy of our times.

'Ananthamurthy's narrative style which balances itself between suggestion and description, his vividness in portraying even minor characters, his profound understanding of human dilemmas and of social and political evil that overpowers even idealists, and his ominous intimations of an impending tragedy in our collective life – *Avasthe* beautifully combines all these elements in what is undoubtedly a masterpiece that will continue to speak to generations.'

– K. SATCHIDANANDAN

'U.R. Ananthamurthy was one of the greatest Indian writers of the last century, as much a master of literary form as an original thinker. *Avasthe*, a complex novel now assiduously Englished, is a bracing reminder of how deftly he fused his tremendous intellectual power and political passion with his fine moral imagination.'

– PANKAJ MISHRA

'The three hungers of our time that U.R. Ananthamurthy often spoke of – modernity, equality and spirituality – are manifest here in all their sharp, serrated tensions. Through the hands of a master novelist, *Avasthe* lays open the question of whether those qualities can ever come together. It explores a landscape of hermits and politicians, village and city, power and fragility, in all its ambiguities. *Avasthe* brings us something we may have lost – the novel of ideas – where crucial questions are given life.'

– SHARMISTHA MOHANTY

Avasthe

A Novel

U.R. Ananthamurthy

Translated from the Kannada
by Narayan Hegde

HARPER**PERENNIAL**

An Imprint of HarperCollins *Publishers*

HARPERPERENNIAL

First published in English in India by Harper Perennial 2020
An imprint of HarperCollins *Publishers*
4th Floor, Tower A, Building No. 10, DLF Cyber City,
DLF Phase II, Gurugram, Haryana – 122002
www.harpercollins.co.in

First published in Kannada as *Avasthe* in 1978
This edition published in India by Harper Perennial 2024

2 4 6 8 10 9 7 5 3 1

Originally published in Kannada as *Avasthe* © Esther Ananthamurthy 1978
English translation © Narayan Hegde 2020, 2024
Afterword © Prayaag Akbar 2020, 2024

P-ISBN: 978-93-5699-152-1
E-ISBN: 978-93-9032-783-6

This is a work of fiction and all characters and incidents described in this book are the product of the author's imagination. Any resemblance to actual persons, living or dead, is entirely coincidental.

U.R. Ananthamurthy asserts the moral right
to be identified as the author of this work.

For sale in the Indian subcontinent only

All rights reserved. No part of this publication may be reproduced, stored in a retrieval system, or transmitted, in any form or by any means, electronic, mechanical, photocopying, recording or otherwise, without the prior permission of the publishers.

Typeset in 12/16.2 Arno Pro at
Manipal Technologies Limited, Manipal

Printed and bound at
Thomson Press (India) Ltd

FSC
www.fsc.org
MIX
Paper from
responsible sources
FSC® C010615

This book is produced from independently certified FSC® paper
to ensure responsible forest management.

Dedicated to dear friends
J.H. Patel
and
S. Venkatram

To the Reader

This novel came to me over a period of about thirty days. I received each day's instalment as a daan, a gift. I am satisfied if it brings you even the slightest of the pleasure which the act of writing brought me.

My dear friend K.V. Subbanna will publish the book in his Akshara Prakashana series. I am grateful to him.

U.R. Ananthamurthy
28 August 1978
First edition

Avastha:

1. The specific order of life as the body ages; infancy, childhood, youth, and so on.

2. Condition, state of being.

3. Effect of time; according to Yaska, a fifth-century Sanskrit scholar, there are six transformational states of being – birth, existence, growth, maturing, decline, and extinction.

Stated in the *Yogashastra* (of Patanjali) are five states of being: ignorance, egotism, passion, hate, and attachment.

According to the Sankhya school of thought, there are three kinds of being: not arrived, manifested, and enlightened.

Sabadarthakaustubhah (Sanskrit–Kannada Dictionary),
Sahitya Vidwan Sri Chakravarti Srinivasa Gopalacharya

Part One

There he lies dying, not yet fifty years old. One might guess at his state of mind as he reminisces while battling death. In his boyhood, Krishnappa Gowda used to be a swimmer. When the river rose in flood, he would jump in and swim all the way across. Once, he and his friend went swimming like this. Just when he had swum halfway across the river, with his friend about a yard out, Krishnappa's arms tired and he could swim no further. 'My friend, I can't swim any more, I'm drowning, you go ahead,' he shouted quickly and went under. His courageous friend – his name was Hanumanayaka – managed to save him. He had felt sure he was dying, but in that moment his mind was totally calm, unperturbed. Remembering it now in his paralysed state, Krishnappa's big eyes fill with tears.

He was short-tempered. Once, when he was in high school, he went to a watch-repairer's shop to fetch a friend's watch. The watch-repairer, the shop's owner, knew Krishnappa well and resented that a poor boy like him went about with a superior air. Magnifying glass tucked in one eye, looking at him from the corner of the other, he said to Krishnappa, 'Do you expect me to hand the watch over, just on trust?'

'Watch out, mister! You talk like that one more time, and I'll smash this glass case of yours to pieces.'

'You know what a poor man's pride will get him? Only broken teeth!' snapped the watch-repairer, pecking at something with a pair of tweezers. Right away, Krishnappa snatched up the glass case with the repair tools and scattered parts of watches, threw it to the ground, shattering it to bits, and walked off. He had such a bad temper, it would scare anyone.

When he is angry now, the most that might happen is that his lips quiver, his nostrils dilate, and his eyes well up. It is sad to see this Durvasa lying in bed, unable to move. Sometimes, he picks up the stick by his side and tries to hit his wife. As for her, she is driven crazy, having to care for a sick husband, slogging at that bank where she is a clerk, looking after a five-year-old daughter who sits in a corner whining and dripping snot. Her hair is always in disarray. 'Dump this empty pride of yours in the kitchen fire,' she once told him, and pinched her daughter's face until the child's lips had blood.

Despite the daily turmoil, it is not that Krishnappa's mind cannot regain its poise. He narrates the story of his earlier life to the simple-minded Nagesh, who is there every day to take down these dictations. It does not much concern him whether the young man is able to grasp the material of his memoirs. Their narration is, for Krishnappa, a means of making sense of his present state.

As a young boy, Krishnappa had to work as a cowherd. Head draped in a coarse blanket, a sickle in one hand and a flute in the other, he would walk through the village, rounding up the cattle, and his charges gathered, he would head to the grazing fields.

He talks about this as though only he can mine its profound meaning. Now that he is dying, does he feel sometimes that something mystical entered his life? Is such a belief necessary in order to transcend the banality of the present? It's hard to say. Intellectually, Krishnappa is an atheist. Yet, he talks about the god-crazed mystics of the land, such as Kabir, Nanak, Allama, Meera and Paramahamsa in a way that is admiring, mocking and sceptical all at once. He jokes about his feeling of oneness with them. It is hard to say what his overall outlook is.

He harks back to those boyhood years.

At the crack of dawn, he would go to the front of each house, untether the cattle, take them to the hillside or to the river or to the grassy meadows, and bring them back with the fall of dusk. He tries to remember the thoughts that came to his mind under the tree, watching the cattle with lazy eyes, playing a fanciful tune on a bamboo flute.

And suddenly, an incident of some significance appears before his eyes. But he prefaces its narration with a laugh: 'Please, young man, do not think that I was having a grand time of it. If the cows happened to see a green field of standing paddy, I was in trouble. Before you knew it, they would have crashed the fences and trampled the crop. All alone, in driving rain, I would helplessly steer the cattle. In the end, there was nothing for it but to give up and sit dumbstruck, thinking of the beating that was sure to come.' His expression bears the fear and the pain he felt. At this point, he remembers Maheshwarayya who freed him from the drudgery of being a boy cowherd.

No one knows who Maheshwarayya was or where he was from. Let's say he moved from somewhere to this new place. The first thing he did was set up a tidy house. Although he lived alone, he kept a cook. But he would wash his own clothes. You should have heard him recite Kalidasa's poetry in Sanskrit, or his classical Hindustani style singing. A great pleasure-loving man he was. His handlebar moustache above lips that were reddened from chewing betel leaf, the glittering diamond studs in his ears, his closed-collar coat, the pure white dhoti that he wore elegantly, the silver-handled cane in his grip, and his serene demeanour, Krishnappa describes these and adds that he was also a great ascetic. Though Maheshwarayya himself would not have been so open, it is Krishnappa's guess that he had left home upon coming to know of his wife's taking a lover. After letting his wife have a part of the estate, Maheshwarayya, who was a millionaire, put the rest in the bank, retired from everything, and set out wandering from place to place. He read all the time.

The man was a visionary who knew the past, the present, and the future. Let's say he arrived at a house. Upon sitting down, suddenly, he would let out a cry: 'Bho!' Then there would settle an uneasy look on his face. Though he knew a sense of foreboding had come over him, he wouldn't say more, no matter how much his host begged. Later, he would whisper his misgivings in Krishnappa's ear. People avoided running into him for fear he might blurt out 'Bho!' It was so spontaneous that he couldn't help it. That is why he would sometimes refuse invitations. To Krishnappa, he would say, 'I don't know what disaster awaits that poor man – I won't go to his house.' Sadly, though Maheshwarayya could foretell the future, he rarely saw any good in it. The one time it was different, he saw in Krishnappa's future something good. This is how it went:

The boy Krishnappa, in his dirty shorts and shirt, was sitting under a peepul tree on the riverbank. The paddy had been harvested, he was not worried about the cattle straying into people's fields. With the murmur of the flowing river and the tinkling of the cowbells, Krishnappa must have felt blissful, perhaps more blissful than usual. Instead of playing the bamboo flute, that day he felt like singing the lines from Kumaravyasa's *Bharata*. He had studied only up to the fourth standard, and so it was not something he had read while at school. He had picked it up from listening to the old brahmin Joisa, who was his teacher. That day, as he got carried away, he sang with great feeling. Not far from where he was sitting, Maheshwarayya, who had been camping out in a nearby town, was washing his coat in the river. How he happened to be at that very spot that day is a wonder. It seems earlier that day, when he was walking in the market, he was stopped by a retired schoolteacher who had gone somewhat crazy. The man asked Maheshwarayya for his coat. 'Of course, you can have it,' Maheshwarayya told him, 'but because I have worn it, I want to wash it before giving it to you.' He bought a bar of soap and came to this riverbank, walking two miles from the town.

Maheshwarayya stood before the singing boy and said, 'Bho!' Embarrassed, Krishnappa stopped. 'Hey, boy! After you are done with the cattle, come back here in the evening and wait for me,' Maheshwarayya said, the coat dripping in his hand while he looked distractedly into the distance. He walked away, wringing the coat, and Krishnappa now remembers there were two flamboyant parrots in the guava tree across from where he was sitting under the peepul. He also remembers that he had never seen the bird in such unusual colours before.

In the evening, Krishnappa waited. Maheshwarayya arrived, swinging his walking stick. 'What a dumb boy! All this time, you haven't understood who you are, have you? Come with me,' he said, and they went directly to where Krishnappa lived. His mother lived with her elder brother in his house, doing chores for him and his wife, chores such as grinding batter for kadubu, cooking the cattle feed, gathering leaves and twigs from the forest for the compost, all the while being nagged by the brother's wife. Krishnappa's father had died.

When he saw Maheshwarayya, the gold rings on his fingers, the gold studs in his ears, and that silver-capped cane in his hand, Krishnappa's uncle stood up in awe.

'How stupid you people are!' Maheshwarayya scolded the house roundly. 'You have here a precious gem in your home, and you don't have the eyes to see it!'

He gave them some money and made arrangements for Krishnappa to board in a student hostel which was ten miles away, so that he could go to a school. After setting up the fund for his schooling expenses, Maheshwarayya disappeared. Once a year, he visited the boy to find out how he was doing.

That is how Krishnappa was able to get an education all the way up to a BA.

'Maheshwarayya remained a mystery to me even after I got to be on familiar terms with him,' he says, remembering those days. 'Whenever I was in some difficulty, he would appear as if from nowhere. He was there when I went to prison, or sometimes when I was down with fever or something. When I stood for election the first time, he gave me a thousand rupees for the expenses. He would arrive in a new place and start living there. Then, just as easily, he would leave that place, giving away household items such as the furniture to strangers. The man was peculiar! Even to this day, I don't know what his caste is or what community he comes from. He could be a brahmin or a Lingayat, guessing from the fact that he was pleased by my vegetarianism. He was so decent towards women from respectable families that he would not look straight at them. But he had a fancy for prostitutes. There was not a single naughty poem from Sanskrit literature that he did not know. Politics did not interest him at all. Extraordinary man!'

No matter how hard you may have to struggle, Krishnappa remembers Maheshwarayya saying, you must go back to live in your own place.

Krishnappa's school was in the town not far from his village. He was, after all, from a poor family. The money from Maheshwarayya put him in school, but it did not staunch his humiliation. The hostel warden, a wealthy landowner, heaped him with scorn. Krishnappa's confidence made people feel as if he were poking his finger in their eyes.

When there is a gap between what we are and what we aspire to be, before our mask can become our face, what struggles unfold. Krishnappa illustrates this with many events from his life. He is near death, but there comes no relief. He saddens when his poor wife, after a beating, her hair dishevelled, grumbles from the kitchen: 'He thinks he's a big leader! He wants to make a revolution! First let him stop beating his wife, then we'll see!' What happened to the sense of humour that Maheshwarayya had taught me to tap as a means of keeping my ego in check? Has it gone from me, now that my body has lost its vigour?

Once, for some since-obscured minor offence, the warden of the hostel threatened to thrash Krishnappa with a cane. Clenching his teeth as if to kill the man, Krishnappa grabbed the cane and faced him, a fierce Rudra, while all the other boys looked on. The man was puny and was, by nature, timid. Watching that pockmarked face, the sunken eyes, the chin pointing up, and the screechy voice shouting orders, Krishnappa was overcome with disgust. All the other boys who had accepted him as their leader stood around in hushed anticipation. Krishnappa turned his back towards the warden, lowered his shorts, and with his finger pointing to a ripe red boil on his arse, turned his head, saying, 'Please, sir, hit me anywhere except where I have this boil,' and offered his backside. The boys burst into loud laughter. It left the warden shaking with humiliation and rage, utter contempt in the eyes around him. Scared, he scurried away. In this manner, Krishnappa often defied the tyranny of wealth and status.

'Do you know there is a tiger in you!' Maheshwarayya used to say. He was quietly a devotee of Durga, the fierce goddess. Sometimes, he would seek a place no one knew about and lose himself to worship, sometimes for months. Krishnappa was witness to one such possession. 'You must ride the tiger,' Maheshwarayya exhorted. At that time, Krishnappa had tried to be sceptical about this man with his red silk madi dhoti, a large dot of kumkum on his forehead, his moist hair now left to grow long for the worship and thrown over the shoulder, his eyes shining with the intensity of his devotion for the goddess. Krishnappa was incapable of worshipping any god or goddess. But he needed, didn't he, to gain the confidence of Maheshwarayya who was capable of making his mask his face? And so, to encounter the mystical, setting aside his scepticism, he listened to Maheshwarayya attentively. With a view to reforming and remoulding him, Maheshwarayya would even rebuke him at times. Thanks to his disapproving comments, Krishnappa, who was in the habit of constantly preening before the mirror, was in the end cured of his self-love.

At times laughing, at times roaring, the tiger within Krishnappa now sprang about. By degrees, he acquired the moral rectitude that would make wrongdoers feel as if they were vermin. He did, after all, make a name for himself as the leader of the opposition in the State Assembly, didn't he? He has enemies, filthy scoundrels who try by all means to silence him. This has made it necessary for Krishnappa to live his life with his teeth always gritted.

Maybe that is why Maheshwarayya, who never became too involved with society, has remained dear to Krishnappa. Krishnappa has been troubled by the question: when corruption is so ingrained in human nature, isn't it absurd to look for absolute purity in daily life?

He constantly tries not to be drowned in the politics of budgets, public projects, bribery, promotions, salary raises, transfers, jobs, and so on. He dreams of revolution, but is aware that his revolutionary acts so far have been piecemeal. Lately, even Maheshwarayya hasn't been around to buoy him up. One has to be either a hot-headed demagogue or a recluse who has turned one's back on society. That he can talk contemptuously of the corrupt makes him pleased with himself, but it also worries him that deriving such pleasure has now become a habit with him. When your rage has changed nothing around you, is it any wonder that it becomes a mere habit? For the pain caused by such indignation, for the venting of that passion, Krishnappa tells himself, the poetry of half-crazed men like Kabir and Allama is a much better means than politics.

But Krishnappa had failed in his attempts to become a writer. When he sat down with a sheet of paper in front of him, he found he couldn't go any further after writing half a sentence in his elegant hand: 'As he was walking one morning, in the harvest season, carrying on his head a basket filled with shit, an untouchable Holeya named Kariya ...' Could it go something like: 'As he was walking, he seethed with an anger that could have burned away the filth of the world'? But to be able to write like that, one should either have genuinely felt that anger in one's own life or one should have the gift of words to make it seem authentic. Krishnappa used to scoff at poets, saying that those who are not capable of action seek to spend their frustration on words. Detecting envy here, Maheshwarayya had admonished him. 'If you have what it takes to set the world on fire, go ahead and do it. Just don't mock the goddess of the word.' Maheshwarayya was of the view that the word, sheltered and tended like the tongue of a flame, was better than rage spilt in scorn everywhere. But Krishnappa knows that his words stick to his ego, that they will burst all over his body like boils from the heat of his bile.

* * *

There was a time when, like a snake sloughing off its skin, Krishnappa suffered for the transformation and even went crazy. He was studying in the intermediate college but could have been twenty-five years old, for who knew the date of his birth? If you asked his illiterate mother, she was likely to say that it was that year of the flood. Anyway, Krishnappa, being poor, was a free boarder in a hostel set aside for students of his caste. He had become the leader of the rich boys in the hostel, nevertheless. The boys had chipped in to let him have a room all to himself, a privilege only he enjoyed. Once, Krishnappa came down with a high fever. A loyal follower of his, a rich boy, was looking after him. Gurappa was the boy's name. Krishnappa asked him for a new mattress. He knew that Gurappa was somewhat stingy, so he explained at some length the kind of mattress he wanted: 'Listen, Gurappa, I want the mattress to be thick, like a box. And it should be edged with a border of a different colour. Do you understand?' Gurappa said, 'Hmm,' and went off to have the mattress made. Krishnappa was delirious with fever when he ran his hand over the side of the new mattress. 'It feels curved like a snake's head. I wanted it flat like a box, a box!' He tried to get up from the bed, and opening his eyes with difficulty, glared at Gurappa. Gurappa's explanation that the mattress was exactly as he was told made Krishnappa angrier. He didn't want a mattress at all, he said, and moved to the bare floor. Fearing that he might catch a cold, Gurappa pleaded with him, but he would not be budged. When Gurappa had a fever a few months before, Krishnappa had stayed at his bedside, putting cold compresses to his forehead and cleaning up his vomit. Gurappa was so grateful that he had begun to almost worship Krishnappa. Yet now, Krishnappa suspected, maybe a new mattress was a waste of money for stingy Gurappa, or maybe he had become bold, thinking that a delirious man need not be taken seriously. Krishnappa was quite nettled by this pettiness he perceived. Gurappa had another mattress made and begged him again, and even then Krishnappa refused. He even refused to sleep in his old bed. Instead, he lay on a palm-leaf mat on the floor. With a sad face, Gurappa sat beside him and attended to his friend, yet not once did Krishnappa turn to address him.

When the fever came down a little, he left to convalesce in the home of his uncle's eldest son. To get there, first he would have to catch a train, travel thirty miles by it, and then get on the only bus, which came at no set time. After getting off the train, he walked up to a roadside hotel and lay down on a bench to wait for the bus. He ran a mild fever. The hotel owner saw Krishnappa lying on the bench. Scratching his stubble, his mouth filling with saliva from chewing tobacco, he made a sign to Krishnappa to get up. Krishnappa only stared at him. The man got angry. He went and spat out his wad, and returned.

'Hey, get up or else I will have you thrown out,' he said.

Staring steadily, Krishnappa said in a calm voice, 'I have a fever. Outside, it is too hot in the sun. Please let me sleep here until the bus comes.' The gentleness of his voice was absent from his eyes.

'Hey, someone there,' the fellow ordered one of his serving boys, 'throw him out of here. This hotel is not a shelter for homeless bastards.'

A boy came around and yanked out the travel trunk from under Krishnappa's head. The owner grabbed it and threw it to the ground, spilling its contents in the afternoon sun. 'I'm warning you! Don't touch me,' Krishnappa said when the man made to grab him, and backed away on unsteady legs. Straightening his sleeves, he quietly put his belongings back in the trunk. He sat on it in the burning sun, staring at the hotel building, and like one notoriously irascible young rishi of ancient times, said coolly, 'This place will burn down – within a month.' The hotel owner spat dismissively. Krishnappa gave him a pitying smile...

He has retained that power for making pronouncements. Too weak to walk, he arranged to be carried into the Legislative Assembly in a chair, and without looking at anyone in particular, proclaimed in a raised voice, 'This is my prophecy, whether anyone heeds it or not is unimportant to me: the poor will rise up in indignation, they will burn down your houses.' Treating this as entertaining news, the editors of the daily newspapers printed it in a box with an exclamation mark at the end. Those who did, in fact, hear him say these words with that serious face and in that grave voice of his didn't find them funny. But in the real world, where stories of people's daily struggles are portrayed as optimistic, these words in print may have seemed ridiculous, appeared to be the ranting of an egotistical man. Krishnappa is aware of this and struggles, despite his weakened body, to keep his frustration and anger sharp for the time when the poor will rise up in revolt.

Krishnappa's cousin, Rangappa, was a lowly office clerk who made a living by taking petty bribes. He had eight young children to feed.

Savitramma was mistress of a house that had just two rooms and a country-style tile roof which leaked. She had a cold all the time, and she would wipe the snot off her hand on the wall while serving her husband and Krishnappa their food. Always grumbling, the woman unashamedly served thick, creamy buttermilk to her husband and a thin watered-down version of it to Krishnappa. His angry glare failed to frighten her. If only he didn't have to come to this town for his treatment, he thought, he would have gone to his village and been with his mother. From her kitchen, Savitramma would watch him lying idly in the room where the children slept. She could be heard issuing taunts about his fancy illness that required him to have rice rather than the plain finger-millet mudde she cooked for everyone else. She would mutter on, cursing her poverty in her usual sing-song, all the while banging pots.

Krishnappa realized that he had no way to cope with the meanness around him except to retreat deep into silence. He no longer looked down on Savitramma for being one of so many wretched women who toiled daily, cleaning the urinating, defecating children, putting food in front of hungry and demanding husbands, and keeping the dusty houses swept. He stopped glowering at her and answering back. He became kind to her so that her pettiness could not overpower his tremulous body and mind. It went on like this for some time until two events in the course of one day transformed Krishnappa in a curious way.

Krishnappa was in the habit of writing a diary. During her grumbling fits, Savitramma would find him writing tiny, round letters in his notebook, looking pleased. Bemused, and not a little annoyed, she would stand and watch him. To that illiterate woman, Krishnappa's absorption made what he was doing seem a ritual of sorcery. One morning, he was still asleep when she took the notebook and flung it on the fire in the bathing corner. If challenged, she was going to say that there was no cow dung and so she used the notebook to heat the water.

Upon waking up, Krishnappa brushed his teeth with a mango leaf, came inside and asked, 'Where's my notebook?' He must have known, for he went back out to the fireplace in the bathing corner and found there a charred piece of the cardboard that used to be the notebook's cover. Holding it in his hand, he confronted Savitramma, silently seething at her. In an innocent voice, Savitramma said, 'There was no cow dung.' He could have killed her there, but he stood stock still, tears threatening his eyes, tears he didn't want Savitramma to see lest they provoke her pity. So he went away and lay down in bed and closed his eyes. Feelings he didn't quite understand surged within him. Pettiness would surely destroy him, and he would be powerless before it. He decided to cut his finger to prove to himself that he was stronger than these people. He fetched his razor blade from the trunk and got ready to inflict the wound, when a woman who was a neighbour came rushing into the house. 'Did you hear, Savitramma? It seems a hotel caught fire and burned down in Arasalu! They say that the owner, that Udupa, got burnt all over and has been admitted to the hospital.'

When he heard that, Krishnappa remembered the curse he had pronounced. Not a month, a month and ten days. But that small detail did not disappoint him. I was born with the divine aspect, and as it becomes more and more manifest, I will be god myself, he thought. He laughed aloud, and with the neighbour and Savitramma looking on, he sliced off his little toe as if he were sharpening a pencil. Blood oozed, but he was laughing.

That was the onset of Krishnappa's madness. Sitting on the floor inside the house, he drew, like Maheshwarayya used to, an elaborate mandala and filled it with kumkum and turmeric. In the centre, he installed the Devi, the mother goddess, by placing a brightly polished pot. With nothing on except a loincloth, he unfolded the *Saundarya Lahari* given to him by Maheshwarayya and sat down with it. Savitramma was appalled that Krishnappa, a shudra, was reciting mantras that were forbidden to him. As his voice rose in perfect intonation, she stood by, dazed. When the children returned from school, she asked them to use the backyard door and forbade them from going to him. Her husband, too, became frightened when he saw Krishnappa sitting there like a man possessed. When Krishnappa broke off in the middle of his puja and ordered him to it, he went quickly to fetch mango leaves and strung them up in festoons.

No one dared approach the inner area of the house, where the worship carried on. For the next three days, uttering not a single word of complaint, Savitramma bathed daily to purify herself, procured the materials needed for the puja, and cooked payasa and kosambari to offer the goddess. In the neighbourhood, no one knew what to do in such an unanticipated situation. Fellow clerks in Rangappa's office, the ones who were brahmins, warned of bad things to come. Others argued that it was impossible for one who is not a brahmin to summon the goddess into a house.

There was speculation about Maheshwarayya who had initiated Krishnappa into mystical rites, but no one had a clear answer about his caste. One co-worker in the office, who had some knowledge of the mantras, let it be known that if the rites Krishnappa was practising were of the Bengal Shakta sect, misfortune was sure to befall the household. This man went with Rangappa to his house, and standing outside, put his ear to the mantras emanating from within. He shook his head – yes, this was definitely a tantric rite. Rangappa asked him, appealing with folded hands, 'Tell me, please. Is there any way to stall the calamity?' 'There is,' he replied, 'I'll tell you. Now that the deity has been summoned and installed, it must be seen off with proper rites. You see, all this – sorcery and magic spells – in the end, destroys the practitioners themselves.' Seeing that the man's fear was in earnest, Rangappa got alarmed.

Krishnappa didn't sleep. Three times a day, he would empty over himself the water he had drawn from the well, only to sit down again to his chanting. Day and night, with no sleep, he pressed on. He only ate a little payasa from the offering. Rangappa would walk some four miles every day to collect a basketful of red hibiscus, the goddess's favourite flower. For the three days that the ritual lasted, the household saw to Krishnappa's wishes. It is incomprehensible today for Krishnappa, who consciously rejects the worship of deities. What he remembers is this: he felt separate from his physical body at the end of his three days of worshipping the Devi.

He stopped then. Getting up, he took off his loincloth and walked out into the street naked. People watched him half in fear and half in veneration, and it made his madness worse. He walked away until, outside the town, he sat down on a stone seat reserved for the Ganapati idol.

Krishnappa doesn't remember what happened next. Who knows from where Maheshwarayya appeared and what treatment was administered – in the end, Krishnappa was cured.

* * *

Madness or not, Krishnappa is capable of such ecstasy even now when he lies in bed waiting for the end. There was always something in him that made it impossible for people to treat him disrespectfully. His name, recorded as 'Krishnappa Gowda', proclaimed his caste.

Yet it presented his teachers with a dilemma, because calling him 'Krishnappa Gowda' would be to call him by his shudra caste name. But to call him 'Krishnappa' would suggest too much familiarity. So everyone called him 'Gowdre' – Mr Gowda – as if he had no name of his own.

He could transcend his limitations and astound everyone. Once, when he was in the Assembly reading from a prepared speech, the governor failed to express concern for a famine that gripped the state and Krishnappa threw a copy of the speech to the floor and stomped on it. As he stood there like an angry god, at first his fellow legislators didn't know what to do. After a few minutes, they began clamouring, 'He has insulted the prestige of the Assembly!' and so on, and expelled him. It was Krishnappa's belief that only crooks need be polite. But if he ever learned that someone he knew was ill, even a political enemy, he would go to his bedside, taking him some fruits. The fact that Krishnappa had come to see him would make the sick person very pleased.

One morning, Krishnappa felt the urge to relieve himself, but he was not able to get out of bed. He called to Sita for the bedpan. She must have been in her bath. Being weak, he couldn't control his bladder and peed in bed. When she came out of the bath and saw his downcast face, she asked, 'Now what happened?' Krishnappa didn't have to tell her, she could tell from the smell. The thought of her relishing his misfortune made him angry. His wife quickly lifted him, and moving him to another bed, said, 'You can't stand my being around. Tell me, who else would have cleaned your piss and shit? That woman, the one you say was waiting for you to marry her, do you think she would have done this for you? Or would that Lucy or Pucy with whom you were carrying on an affair have done it?' Krishnappa thought his wife was being conciliatory with him, which made him angrier. She was gaining the upper hand over him through her nursing.

He had told her about his relationships with Gowri Deshpande and Lucina. In telling her, he had tried to make her accommodating and broadminded. But when he talks of this stuff, she has no reaction except to say, 'I don't understand any of these things. Did you take your medicine in the afternoon?' Or she tells him that the woman next door has invited her to see a matinee show and she'd better be on her way. Her world is confined to everyday household affairs, or at the most, the affairs of her fellow workers in the bank – such as someone getting married, their children, someone's munji ceremony, or someone giving birth.

Krishnappa had one child, a daughter, with Sita the year they were married, and thereafter he was not able to have physical relations with her any more. But now, from bathing to cleaning him when he soiled himself, it was she who did everything for him. Krishnappa was aware that she was winning over him. Lately, her enduring him quietly when he dealt with her cruelly made him fear that he was becoming hollow within himself.

From before, from the beginning, she had been winning. If she hadn't, he would hardly have tried to gain her respect by telling her about Lucina and Gowri. All the skills of foreplay he employed to impress on her the sophistication of his body and mind were made ludicrous by her dumbness. Watching him undress slowly, discarding the dhoti then the shirt, and becoming bored with his talk, she would laugh and say in a pitying way, 'Hurry up. Don't keep me waiting. I have to wake up early and get to work, don't I?' At that moment, Krishnappa would feel his desire for her slip away. He had told her about Savitramma burning his diary, and she had asked in surprise, 'What can possibly be in a diary that is so important?' Basically, I must be of her level or else would I have married her? I am being brought down to the level I really belong to! In despair, he would fall asleep. At other times, his desire drove him to drink, and he would drink hard before getting intimate with her.

* * *

It was in his final year of college, when he was completing his BA, that his friendship with Gowri began. Krishnappa was the older by seven or eight years, if one were conservative, on account of his delayed schooling. He had been to jail in the national freedom movements of 1942 and 1947, and his legend stood established, especially among female students. The ones who were particularly sensitive and knew about his short temper, pride and his mad phase, held him in higher regard than they did their teachers. He rarely attended classes, and when he did even the teachers took their teaching more seriously, omitting their usual silly jokes. He didn't bother with tests or sitting exams, had an extraordinary intellect, was an older, mature person given to independent thinking – all this made his teachers very uneasy.

Krishnappa was of a dark, muscular build. He would wear a sparkling dhoti and a jubba of khadi to college. In that all-white attire, he would appear a finely chiselled dark statue. When he glowered in anger, his otherwise serene face grew harsh and fearsome. His voice was soft yet robust, like a singer's. The girls called him, in secret, the African prince. 'The prince is here today, see?' the girls said cheerily whenever they saw him in class, which was not often.

Gowri Deshpande was known in the college as a dancer and a singer, and as the best student in her class. Some clever girls who had guessed that she liked Krishnappa used to tease her by calling her Radha. Not to her face, because Gowri was never that close to anyone and kept to herself much of the time. The girls found her intriguing for a reason. It was known that her mother, who had left her husband, was the kept mistress of the wealthy betel-nut merchant Nanjappa. But Gowri's demeanour was so dignified, they could not rightly condescend to her.

That wealthy man Nanjappa had built Anasuyabayi, Gowri's mother, a bungalow and provided a car and driver for her use. This house, with its large compound and roses growing in it, was well known in the town. Anasuyabayi was hardly seen outside her house, but her beauty was praised by even those who had never laid eyes on her. If Gowri was so beautiful, went the speculation, how much more beautiful should her mother be! Though her house was on the outskirts, Anasuyabayi would never make the trip into town in her car. She used the car only to go out of town, to the Kemmannu Gundi resort or Mangalore city. The car ferried Gowri Deshpande to the college and back daily, which made the girls envious. They often gossiped: her last name being Deshpande, she must have a father by that name somewhere. They pitied that, instead of her father, she was made to live with the mother's paramour. They sneered that, despite being rich, she danced in public shamelessly. At the same time, they beheld in awe the way she carried herself.

Gowri behaved as if there was nothing she shared with their world. Wearing no jewellery, in a white sari and a white blouse, a single white rose tucked in her long black braid, she would come to the class and sit looking serious. Between lessons, she would take herself to the ladies' lounge to read a book. When the girls talked among themselves, they used easily the familiar form of addressing each other in the singular. If someone addressed her in this way, she would respond politely in the formal, plural pronoun, and thus, maintain her distance. Krishnappa, though he hadn't spoken to her, felt a kind of kinship with her.

One evening, Krishnappa was walking by himself near the college. The volleyball team was returning home after a game. As the rest of them watched, a burly man, who was the team captain, scribbled something on the wall. Krishnappa looked up in their direction when he heard them laugh. The burly chap was Ramu. In the college, he was known as a tough guy. More or less Krishnappa's age and the son of a prominent rice-mill owner, he was jealous of Krishnappa's growing repute. Krishnappa wouldn't care to so much as look at the rowdy students. For him, there was no one at his level in the college. The students had no strategy for someone like him, who showed no interest in competing with anyone.

Gowri, a prostitute's daughter! What do you charge for a kiss? Ramu stood back to admire what he had written in large letters. Krishnappa went up to him and said in his serious, deep voice, 'Wipe off what you have there.'

For a moment, Ramu didn't know what to say.

'How do you know it's I who wrote it?' he said weakly, using the formal 'you'. He said it with a sneer so that his cronies would appreciate his smart-alecky answer.

'I saw you at it,' Krishnappa said, suppressing his anger, not bothering with formality.

Ramu was a wrestler. He had grown a big moustache. Perhaps, out of envy, he secretly wished to be close to Krishnappa. Like any experienced wrestler, he thought that when you fight a strong rival you gain his friendship as an equal. But Krishnappa only looked down on him and seemed unwilling to become his pal by exchanging blows.

Ramu tried to provoke him. 'What is she to you? Your Radha, Mr Krishnappa?'

Krishnappa would hit him now, and Ramu could have his honour restored by beating him up. But he hoped in vain. Krishnappa wet his handkerchief at a nearby tap and began to wipe the writing off the wall.

Ramu waited, to further provoke him. 'Looks like she gives it to you for free,' he said. His companions whistled encouragingly. But Krishnappa started walking away without so much as glancing at them, as if they didn't exist at all. As he walked away, he suspected that they might be writing on the wall again but resisted the urge to look back. Hadn't he got the better of the meanness around him? Let Gowri, too, win in the same way, he thought.

The wall remained bare the next day, and Krishnappa thought that he had won. Then the following morning, in tar, there appeared words like *Gowri gives it to Krishnappa free* and *Krishnappa is Gowri's pimp*. All over the college, people whispered. Once the classes were in session, the attendants erased the tar. Still, the words remained etched. Krishnappa went about as if he was unconcerned, but searched for Gowri's face. He sensed that she looked hurt but not rattled. That evening, he went to her house and rang the bell.

Gowri, who was in the middle of her singing practice, led him inside and made him sit down, not letting him see the joy that had come over her. Krishnappa, though, could sense that she was secretly happy to see him. He felt encouraged, and looking down at the carpet, spoke softly:

'You are the only one in the college who is equal to me. I realized it today.'

Attempting not to look at her, he cast his glance towards the glass coffee table, the pictures of deities on the wall, and the musical instruments strewn around. He looked out of the large window, at the roses in the garden. He regretted that he had cheapened himself by coming over and saying a thing like that.

'Don't mind what I said. It was rather cheap of me to talk like that. It made you cheap as well.'

'Not at all. Please ... sit,' Gowri spoke haltingly. 'It is true my mother left my father when I was a child. She is kept by Mr Nanjappa as his mistress. See, all these things belong to him. Now that you know this, I don't know what you think.' Gowri stood up, turning her face away as though she was trying to hide her anxiety.

'I didn't come here to console you. I think of you as a special person and I have respect for you,' Krishnappa said, getting up.

'My father was one Mr Deshpande. He, too, had kept my mother as his mistress. He went to prison for embezzling money at the bank he worked for. My mother can't be without a man to support her, and so...'

'Now you are testing me, aren't you? It's rather cheap, you know!' Krishnappa said, glaring at Gowri.

Gowri let out a big laugh, relieved. When she laughed like that, she looked impish and it made Krishnappa awkward. He thought he could open himself up to her and say to her that against meanness you either win or you succumb. Her playful nature discouraged him. Gowri saw in his face an expression that seemed to say: I am unfathomable to you.

She said, 'You are quite conceited, aren't you?'

Krishnappa looked away, annoyed. She may be trying to win with me, he thought. Is she asking me seriously or is she teasing me? If she was teasing, his answering her would be vanity. When he arrived at her house, she had on her forehead the sacred ash of vibhuti instead of the usual dot of kumkum, and she was at singing practice. Now, poised like a classical dancer, she stood with her hand on her arched waist.

Seeing him look away, Gowri said, 'I wasn't being funny. My mother is a good person. Nanjappa, too, is a good man. But I live my life outside anyone's reach. I haven't cried in years. That is why I think I too may be conceited, like you.'

Krishnappa's face hardened, his eyes narrowed.

'Would you like to see my mother? She is upstairs. I'll ask her to come down,' Gowri said in the tone of a good host.

'No, please. I wouldn't know what to say. It would be uncomfortable,' he said, looking at Gowri impassively, and placing his hands in his pockets, walked away.

* * *

Back in his room, he wrote a letter.

Dear Shrimathi Gowri Deshpande,

I suspect that you posed the question only to test me, and so I didn't answer. Why should we tell others what we can't say to ourselves when we are alone? There is insincerity in anything that we say out of consideration for others. For that reason, I am against politeness. Politeness is for those who want to make money, who desire popularity, but in a sincere relationship it is a hindrance. I came looking for you because I thought that we could each know the other. But it is quite possible that I, too, was acting out of a weakness that made me seek your sympathy. I am not conceited. I don't think you are either. I may appear to be conceited to those who are victims of their own pettiness.

When I look at a tree, a bird, an animal, a beggar, or anyone else, I only feel different, not above any of them. I show my pride like a serpent that uses its venom when it feels it is being attacked. I am not to blame for my pride – it is the world in which I was born and grew up. Looking at your background, it seems true of you too. The pettiness we see outside is within us as well. Both from outside and within, it conspires to undermine our intensity, against which we must guard constantly. Such a stance may seem vain to genteel ones. But it is inevitable. To remain unaffected by everyday temptations, to be acutely aware of everything that lives and dies around us – that is yoga. Remember the twin concepts – energy and matter.

– Krishnappa

Krishnappa mailed the letter on the way to Kumbarakoppalu, a grubby part of town. Down a narrow, dingy lane, he came to a grocer's shop and looked up. Seeing that the light was on in the room above, he took the rickety stairs that reeked of piss.

'Who is it?' Annaji said in answer to his knock, and after making sure it was Krishnappa, opened the door wearing a jubba. An incense burned in the room so that the stench became bearable. 'Sit down,' Annaji said in English, and showed him to a corner of the bed which was laid on the floor and sat himself down in another corner.

Annaji was a middle-aged, handsome-looking man. He was tall and slim, with a prominent chin and bushy brows. He had grown his hair to shoulder length, which he combed backwards. From the stubble on his face, one might calculate that he had been growing a beard for about a month now. Lighting a Charminar cigarette, Annaji waited for Krishnappa to say something.

Krishnappa noticed a book by Trotsky lying on the bed which Annaji must have been reading. The small room, with its sloping roof of country tiles, had a bed, a trunk, a few books, and nothing else.

Krishnappa withdrew two hundred rupees from his pocket and handed them to Annaji. Annaji, who knew Krishnappa's nature well, pocketed the money without a 'thanks' or otherwise displaying the gratitude he felt.

'Soon, I have to move out of this room,' he said, speaking in English, as he got up and went to the small wooden window that opened on to the street below. Sliding the grimy curtain, he pointed to a man who was standing outside, and said:

'Look, a policeman in civilian clothes! The pig! He's been watching everyone who comes and goes since yesterday.'

'Come and stay with me in my hostel.'

As if to say it wouldn't be safe to do so, Annaji shook his head.

Krishnappa didn't address him as 'Annaji'. He never knew what his real name was, for Annaji was on the run and went by different names in different places. Originally from Maharashtra, he had escaped Portuguese jail in Goa and made his way east to the Telangana region. While he was organizing the farmers in a village there, some of his followers tried to kill a wealthy landowner. They had gone further than Annaji's plan. The landowner, though, only broke a leg. The farmers were charged with attempted murder. The prosecution managed to turn one of the accused men, and the police had the material they needed to incriminate Annaji. In this town, Annaji had managed to find some work giving tuitions in English at four or five houses. He was wanted by the Andhra police under the name R.L. Naik. The Portuguese government in Goa was looking for him under the name P.T. Deshpande and was ready to hang him. Krishnappa never asked to know more of Annaji than what he volunteered. It could be said that for Krishnappa, who was looking for a purpose in life, a man like Annaji who had read hundreds of books on revolution seemed like a mentor, just as Maheshwarayya had.

Wherever Annaji lived, he had a mistress whom he left behind when he moved. Every month, he would send each of them some money. Like the tiger's wound that never heals, his debt kept expanding. Krishnappa would be sent to the post office with the money order. Twenty-five to a tailor's daughter in Kolhapur for her teacher education training; twenty-five to an office clerk in Goa with whom he had fathered a child; twenty-five to the woman he had married when she was still very young who, after giving birth to a son, had gone back to live with her parents in Nagpur. Also, to those poor followers of his who had been lending him money for the past fifteen years. After all, they had to be paid back once in a while. Annaji, thus, was steeped in debt. With no other encumbrances or expensive habits, he could live just on tea and cigarettes and sleep on a straw mat.

Always scrounging around for money, dodging his debtors with lies like 'I'll pay you back next week', Annaji would use all his ingenuity to humbug people. It disgusted Krishnappa. But Annaji was a man who had no regard for his name or reputation. When, at the beginning of their acquaintance, Annaji asked him for money, Krishnappa, who had to raise the money through others, angrily said to him, 'I have respect for you, so never lie to me.' For a few moments, Annaji was stunned. Then, as he started relating the story of his life, Krishnappa told him, 'Never mind. I will collect some money for you every month.' In addition, Annaji made about a hundred and fifty a month from English lessons.

'You are a man totally dedicated to ideology. Why do you get involved in these silly affairs?' Krishnappa had asked without expecting an answer, as if he had posed the question to himself.

'In your conceitedness, you think of yourself as perfect. You are, fundamentally, a fascist,' Annaji said, lighting a Charminar.

The two men were drinking Bombay-style tea in a Muslim hotel. The radio was blaring in the background, and they spoke in raised voices.

'One who lives for the revolution shouldn't give in to infatuations, shouldn't be so bourgeois, preoccupied with matters of money.' Krishnappa had, not so long ago, learned these words from Annaji.

'What you say is right. But even if I keep to myself, women don't leave me alone,' Annaji said, as though it were a mystery to himself. He stood up and started out briskly. Annaji was as sprightly as Krishnappa was languid.

These were probably the most crucial days of Krishnappa's life. Sitting in a park, munching on peanuts, Krishnappa and Annaji would engage in serious discussion. Annaji opened his lesson in politics with a quote from Marx: 'The philosophers have only interpreted the world in various ways; the point, however, is to change it.' Ideas like these had set Krishnappa thinking. Annaji would provoke him with the view that our conscience does not exist as an independent entity but is conditioned by the various factors involved in economic production. Krishnappa, who was firm in his belief that we should not allow ourselves to be defeated by the vagaries of the material world, could hardly agree. Even now, in his paralytic condition, he has his doubts. Back then, he argued:

'That man should transcend his circumstances is not my argument. It's something that I say from personal experience. Anyway. What purpose is accomplished by your organizing the workers and the farmers to demonstrate in the streets? Their wages may increase a little, it may enable each household to buy a radio and stainless-steel utensils. Does it bring change in their lives and the world? The same daily grind, the same struggles, the same problems – will they all go away? On the other hand, people will become more materialistic – thanks to people like you.'

'It's not like that. Now you're talking like an individualist.'

Krishnappa would get annoyed by the way Annaji tried to brush aside his scepticism by tossing out words like 'individualist'. But Annaji would explain patiently:

'It is not that this struggle will stop once we have prepared the poor to strive for improvement in their lives. There is a difference between their aspirations and the selfish desire of our middle class for improving our standard of living. Their aspirations are dynamic. As their aspirations rise, the world itself will have to undergo a change. It is their labour that sustains and drives the society, I hope you know this. The basis of all our progress is this labour of the working class. But it is the capitalist who profits from their labour. It is a system that is supported by exploitation. As they are being exploited, the poor come to realize increasingly that they have no connection with what they grow using their hands. As they begin to understand that it is men who exploit men, they will also realize that, rather than improving the society, they must change the very system that makes their daily life meaningless. A few like me who are from the upper classes may understand it through our conscious effort, but for a sensitive individual like you who comes from the farming class, it comes through your experience. Men like you will, in turn, spread the awareness in others. That is how revolutions happen. To think that we can bring about a revolution just by wishing it is extremely egotistic. It's like the old woman who believed that the dawn occurred because of her cock's crowing. Revolutions occur as part of the society's evolutionary process. We are only the agents of its acceleration, the midwives who facilitate its birth.'

Annaji spoke of such things with a glint in his eye. Looking at a boy pleading with them that they buy his peanuts and jaggery, Krishnappa had said half sceptically, 'You mean to say that even wretched boys like him will rise in indignation and make revolution?'

'Sure. You know of the storming of the Bastille prison when the people of France revolted, don't you?'

'But once the excitement and the fervour of the day cool, the world will become bogged down with its meaningless daily scramble, don't you think?'

'No. With revolution, even daily life becomes creative.'

Annaji's conviction about the infallibility of his way of thinking irritated Krishnappa.

'For every event in life, like birth, death, eating, ploughing, copulating, our Hindu religion has devised a ceremonial ritual. For example, do you know the meaning of our Bhoomi Hunnime festival?' Krishnappa said wearily. But Annaji would analyse even a statement like that:

'There is a difference between your illusions of overthrowing those pointless rituals and invalidating them in reality. As the worker's relationship to production changes, work becomes creative. In your conceitedness, you walk about like a big shot, fancying yourself rising above the mediocrity around you. Go and work among the farmers instead. Organize them for the fight. Think of yourself as the midwife. The real Bhoomi Hunnime is when they become the owners of the land they work.'

Krishnappa knew the different reality of his own experience. Annaji's arguments too appeared reasonable. It perplexed him.

'Do you mean to say, then, that in Russia all labour has become creative?' Krishnappa challenged Annaji.

'Look, it's true that everything that should have happened in Russia hasn't happened. Soon after preparing its people for the revolution, the system itself turned into dictatorship. Revolution is not accomplished overnight. Mistakes happen, but they must be constantly corrected. Look at China now—'

'Get away!' Annaji shouted in English at the boy who was pestering them to buy peanuts, and lit a cigarette. He stuck it in his mouth, rolled up his baggy sleeves, and took out a paper and pencil from his pocket. As he started drawing a map of China and explaining the Long March, Krishnappa said, in an angry voice:

'The communists in our country are traitors. Tell me, why did they side with the British during the Quit India Movement of 1942? I simply cannot see myself pimping for Russia and China.'

Annaji said, without losing patience:

'The communists in our country are impotent, I agree. But I also think it was important to defeat Germany in the Second World War. Yet, I left the party and took part in Gandhi's movement. I know these are all contradictions. Look, Krishnappa, what I want is this: I have seen in you a tremendous hatred for the selfish and the money-grabbing sort. This hatred, this resentment, is an essential motivating factor for the revolution of the dalits. I say this because I feel that you have, more than I do, the grit needed for sowing the seeds of revolution. Right now, my life is all messed up with its petty entanglements. I can't, on my own, free myself from all that. But when the time comes, and when the people of our country are ready for revolution, I know I can free myself from everything and stand by them. In Goa, when the police were ready to shoot me if I took one step further, the people behind me who had come to join the satyagraha got cold feet. Overcoming my cowardice, I took one step forward in defiance of the police and waited for the sound of the gunshot. All those who were hanging back came rushing forward. The police just stood there, unable to shoot. I may exceed the bounds of my bravery in special moments like that. You, on the other hand, should be able to transcend your circumstances every moment. Coming from the farming community, you can pull hundreds of people along with you. And you must do it. It is a proven fact that if you are an individualist by nature, gradually you will lean towards fascism. To avoid it, you should become a man of the masses. We should build a new revolutionary party in this country, one that is aware of the history of exploitation in this land as well as its glory…'

Annaji talked spiritedly, as if possessed. Though he had been moved by the talk, Krishnappa couldn't help expressing his scepticism.

'Why go through all that trouble for people to just go on eating, sleeping and dying?'

Annaji got angry.

'Shut up! Don't let me hear your arrogant talk. Who are you to think that there is something more important than living? Are you god? You whine about the daily life as paltry. What else is there besides living? What task is more important than bringing brightness to that routine living itself? Don't talk like a self-deluding idiot who thinks he can rise above everything by losing himself in some trance or divine ecstasy.'

No one, until now, had sneered at Krishnappa like that. When he said these words, Annaji seemed to him a larger-than-life person. So, respectfully, yet feeling what he was going to say might be irrelevant, he said:

'Look, the two I feel affinity with are Buddha and Christ. Christ said to his mother, "Woman, behold your son!" I like the thinking that lies behind those words. Similarly, I think, the words of our half-crazed Allama, Nanak, Kabir and the like have a profound truth hidden in them. That's why, for one to become entangled in the issues of people's day-to-day lives ...'

Krishnappa stopped mid-flow. He felt that completing what he was saying would oversimplify the real complexity of his thinking.

Annaji didn't say anything. Krishnappa, too, sat quietly. The cool breeze felt good. In the park, there were newly-wed couples, women trying to calm their crying children and their pot-bellied husbands, retired old men who probably quarrelled with their grown-up children. Annaji believes that the lives of these people will get brighter, Krishnappa thought incredulously.

Annaji said softly:

'None of those you talk about stood outside society, Krishnappa. The difference between them and us is that they tried to win the world through their illusion. We will try to win at the factories, in the farms – in the real sense. If you remain authentic, sooner or later, you too will have to think like me.'

* * *

Annaji had decided to move, for the time being, to the home of Channaveerayya where he had been giving private lessons. Krishnappa doubted whether the man in civilian clothes was, in fact, a CID officer. It could very well be Annaji's imagination. He liked to surround himself with mysterious goings-on. Without them, life's routines would be too dull for him. But he seemed really scared that day.

'I am going to turn off the light now and slip out. After a while, have my books and other belongings sent to Channaveerayya's house. Make sure that pig doesn't get suspicious,' Annaji whispered as he turned off the light and left. Krishnappa kept an eye on the man's movements for a while. He too left. Perhaps he was following Annaji, Krishnappa thought. Annaji, who had already anticipated this, had indicated his guerrilla-like plan: instead of going straight to Channaveerayya's house, he would go to the Muslim hotel and eat something there, visit one or two of the houses where he gave private lessons to let them know he would not be coming back for about a month, and then go to Channaveerayya's house taking a roundabout route.

After a short while, the man in civilian clothes appeared again, this time closer. He was thick-necked and had a bald head. He wore a dhoti and a coat. He was buying cigarettes in a shop across the street. Krishnappa watched him closely so that he would be able to recognize him later. In his spotless dhoti, he looked like a betel-nut farmer who had probably come to town to sell his harvest to a middleman, a commission agent. He might be looking for the house of a prostitute which he had been told was somewhere in the neighbourhood, perhaps biding his time to enter when no one was looking. Krishnappa was irked that he was being made to snoop around like this. In all the political protests he had taken part in so far, he had been a follower of Gandhi's principles. Something was wrong with Annaji's kind of politics, which was not practised in the open. He was always plotting and scheming to split the party he was in, through ploys that he called tactics. A political revolution that grew out of such manoeuvring did not appeal to Krishnappa's nature. But Annaji had seemed to him a visionary as well, and he didn't hide anything from Krishnappa.

The man in the coat and dhoti took out a black topi from his pocket and put it on his head. Krishnappa saw him get into a jutka and leave. Once he was out of sight, Krishnappa got a jutka, loaded all of Annaji's belongings on to it, and went to Channaveerayya's house, also taking a roundabout route.

* * *

Channaveerayya was a wealthy man, about thirty years of age. He was a contractor by occupation. He was a member of the municipality and trying to become its president. He was also a member of the town's Rotary Club and was hoping to become its governor so that he could visit America. Not long after Independence, he had joined the Congress party, and turned out in a closed-collar coat and trousers in the party-style, he moved around in a car and became important enough as a leader to gain notice in the newspapers once in a while.

One obstacle between him and his ambitions was his English. He couldn't become the governor of the Rotary Club without it, and he regretted wasting his college years on rowdy activities. Now all his money couldn't extend his sphere of influence beyond this town. Wanting to get close to a man who hobnobbed with police chiefs in the clubs, Annaji went to see Channaveerayya in the first week of his arrival in the district and addressed him in English. He used to be on the editorial staff of the *Statesman* and now, he said, having left the job, he was writing a book. Introducing himself as Annaji S. Katre, he asked Channaveerayya if he, an important man in the town and a Congress leader, could provide material on the freedom fighters of the district for the book.

Channaveerayya heard the entreaty, sitting on the rattan chair in his marble-floored veranda, nodding all the while as if he understood every word. Annaji's fluent English sounded like the English in a radio broadcast. As Annaji went on, Channaveerayya would say 'I see' or 'All right', waiting for the meeting to end. Inside, getting the tea, he said to his wife, 'What is he saying? He talks so fast, like an express train. I can't keep up with him.' Channaveerayya made the admission nonchalantly, with a smile. His wife Uma, the daughter of a magistrate, had been to a convent school. He had acquired her with the power of his wealth, an English-speaking wife for his advancement towards a membership of the Rotary Club. Uma had been listening to Annaji talk while she sat at her embroidery inside. Laying out the biscuits and tea on the dining table, she explained the gist of what he had said and told Channaveerayya to invite him in. Channaveerayya said, 'Come in,' and Annaji entered. He bowed respectfully to Uma, told her, in his broken Kannada, that he used to know Kannada when he was in Kolhapur and that, here in this town, he gave English lessons to a few young men in his spare time. Turning to Channaveerayya, he said, 'Even after getting Independence, our people haven't got over their infatuation with English. I have heard that you are a great orator in Kannada.' He complimented Uma as he drank her tea.

Channaveerayya was delighted at this unexpected advance of friendship from an intellectual. He would, he told himself, show off this man who spoke English so fluently to his Rotary friends. He would, he decided, learn English from him in secret.

Annaji's plan had succeeded better than he had expected. Channaveerayya sent a car every day to fetch him. He would be taking his stroll on the front lawn, chanting his morning prayers; the moment he saw Annaji at the gate, he would greet him with English words of welcome which he had learned; he would then lead him indoors. The conversation in English would continue at the breakfast table. This is excellent! Thank you! Some sugar? How many spoons? The weather is nice today! The conversation would flow on until breakfast was over, all the while Annaji correcting the mistakes in the English Channaveerayya had learnt in college. Uma, who knew the language much better, would serve, enjoying Annaji's refined manners and speech. Educated men like him never came to their house. Those who came were mostly black marketeers, gamblers, that sort. They spoke crudely. Paying no attention to her, they helped themselves to the food and coffee laid out on the table, wiped the dirt and the cow dung from their sandals on the carpet, and left. She had noticed in Annaji a subtle aversion to the opulence of the house. She recognized his revulsion for the wealthy in the enigmatic expressions on his face, though he said nothing. She had begun to suspect that the English lessons, etc., were a ploy and that he was a man of mystery. Annaji, too, would watch, with secret relish, her dusk-complexioned face, her shapely nose and lips, her small but alert eyes, and her cheetah-like build. Without saying a word, he would make her aware that his entire being was keenly absorbing her presence. She felt grateful for the respect he had for her.

Without his telling her, she could guess what he liked. She stopped wearing glossy rayon saris and wore only starched and crisply ironed cotton saris. If she made a special delicacy, she would pack it in a lunchbox and tell her husband to give it to Annaji before he left. Supposedly for her husband, but really for her, he would bring the works of Gorky and Chekhov, which she would read appreciatively.

'I don't get the time to read at all,' Channaveerayya would say in English. 'She will read it every day and tell me about it.' And he would laugh.

Annaji would calmly correct him: 'It's not "She will read it every day". It should be "She reads it every day to me".'

'Yes. Yes. She reads it every day to me. You see, even my friends who are all double graduates do this mistake. Therefore, I have also picked it up,' Channaveerayya would say, lighting a cigarette and offering one to Annaji.

'You must first offer it to me,' Annaji would say with a laugh.

'Excuse me,' Channaveerayya would say in English.

Uma was startled when she realized that Annaji was aware of her noticing all this.

When he began to fear continuing in his room, he had said to Channaveerayya in English, while at breakfast:

'My room is like a pigsty. Especially when it rains cats and dogs, it starts dripping. Sometimes furry caterpillars crawl across the wall like moving rags.'

Is this another lesson in idioms for me, Channaveerayya wondered. Or is Annaji telling me something? Or is it both? Suddenly, he was confused. Stupefied by the fluent phrases, and trying to file them away for the future, he kept listening. Watching her husband listen like an idiot, Uma laughed.

'I need a room to stay. You are a member of the municipality, Mr Channaveerayya. Can you recommend me for a room somewhere?'

Channaveerayya had not yet recovered from his stupor. The shock from the English wore off when he was reminded, to his gratification, that he was a member of the municipality. These words he could understand, for they made him feel important. Annaji sat quietly, enjoying the silly smile on Channaveerayya's face. Uma said, in Kannada:

'Why do you have to stay in that awful room? We have a guest room above our garage. Come and stay until you've found another place.'

'Yes, yes,' Channaveerayya said, collecting himself. Whenever he said 'gyah-rage', Annaji would correct it as 'guhraaj'. But how quickly his wife Uma had caught the correct pronunciation! He felt anger, jealousy, and at the same time, pride that he had such a woman in his possession.

Uma saw to it that the trunk and the bedroll that Krishnappa had brought were carried to the guest room by the servant. Krishnappa wondered at Annaji's good fortune. Annaji's thin cotton mattress was of no use any more. Uma had it stored in the cupboard. She arranged his books on the bookshelf. A teakwood bed with a Dunlop mattress on it, a white bedsheet tucked in on the sides, another bedspread with a print of birds covering the bed. A flask filled with drinking water on the table. Attached bathroom. Carpeted floor. Orange curtains in the windows. In such a room, Annaji's discoloured, dented trunk looked pathetic. Uma noticed it, and it made her smile. She tried to lift it from the side table, but realizing that it was heavy, she got the servant to put it away in the cupboard.

'Annaji will be here after lunch,' Krishnappa said.

There was disappointment on Uma's face. Krishnappa told her that he was leaving. 'Wait,' she said, and had a glass of Bournvita brought to him.

'My husband has gone to the club. He usually comes home late. You may wait, if you want to see him.'

'No,' Krishnappa said, and bowing silently to her, left.

Walking down the steps, he remembered why he had gone to see Annaji. He wanted to tell him about his decision to drop out of college. I'll tell him later, he said to himself. He went back to the hostel and went to bed without supper. He was not able to sleep until the early hours of the morning. All night, he felt a strange anxiety, a kind of anxiety he had not felt before. Early in the morning, when the engines of the lorries that always parked in front of the hostel started up, the noise did not bother him as it usually did. Rather, he found the familiar sound a little comforting even.

* * *

Come morning, Krishnappa woke up with eyes that were red from the lack of sleep. He was a free boarder, but someone or the other, usually a high-school student, brought him his morning coffee in his room. In the hostel, there was a competition of sorts to serve him. After washing his face, Krishnappa sat trying to clear his head, when a boy named Kishorekumar, the son of a rich man, brought him his coffee and quietly put it in front of him. Krishnappa, who was staring out of the window, accepted it and said gratefully to the boy, 'Have you had your coffee? Come and sit.'

He said, 'Gowdre! Some pigs have written all kinds of filthy things about you on the walls! All of us in the hostel are mad at them.'

'Let them write,' said Krishnappa. He had not been asleep most of the night. When could those rogues have come here to write on the walls?

'They have written all kinds of things, disgusting even to read. We don't want you to read it, so some of us are taking it off.'

Krishnappa smiled. He got up to go downstairs with the coffee cup. Kishorekumar tried to take it from him, but Krishnappa wouldn't allow it.

To his fellow students who were whitewashing over the writings on the wall, he said:

'Let it be! Why do you have to get so upset about it?'

The hostel boys were angry with the hooligans of the volleyball team, whom they suspected. Why they were upset became clear to

Krishnappa – the entire student body of the Vokkaliga community would have felt the affront.

'We'll make those sons of whores throw up the sambar-saaru they eat!' said Shamanna, who roamed dashingly on an old motorcycle he owned. Though he was the son of a wealthy landlord, he accorded to Krishnappa the respect due to an intellectual of the community.

'I am thinking of dropping out of college,' Krishnappa said to calm them down.

'Why should you drop out of college? We'll make them crawl at the feet of our sister Gowri, you'll see!' Shamanna said. He was, like most other boys, not averse to whistling at girls, but he called Gowri Deshpande 'sister' because he knew that she regarded Krishnappa with respect. Krishnappa said nothing more and went back to his room to read. But he could not concentrate, his mind was unsettled by vague anxieties. He thought of it as a sign that something beyond his powers was confronting him. Skipping breakfast, he set out to see Annaji, walking slowly.

Though he could hardly understand his anxiety, the silent image of Gowri Deshpande kept coming to mind, and it occurred to him that she was becoming essential to him. Walking through the park, he felt like heading over to her house. To tell her what? To tell her 'I love you'? That would be impossible. Is it because of my pride? He wasn't sure. At least he had begun to recognize that there was a void in him, and no one could fill it but her. He felt anxious that in his helplessness he might just arrive at her door. The writings that had appeared on the walls had seemed to him an attempted assault on his inner dignity by the meanness that surrounded him. To take notice would be beneath him. For all that, the anxiety he was feeling was all the more puzzling.

Sitting on a plush sofa with his legs outstretched, Annaji was smoking a Charminar and talking to Uma. Uma sat on a stool facing him. She was listening, her round face cupped in her palms, looking admiringly at him with her big eyes. Annaji was in the middle of a captivating narration that brought the French Revolution alive right before you, like in the cinema. Krishnappa came in quietly and took another sofa. He looked around, and his eyes were met with the sudden good fortune Annaji had found. A flower vase on the table as well. Uma's eyes gleaming! Annaji had shaved off the month's worth of stubble on his face. Having taken a bath, he had put on a bright dhoti and jubba.

'Mr Channaveerayya has arranged for me to give a talk this evening at the Rotary Club. You should come,' he invited Krishnappa. Uma went off to bring him coffee.

When Krishnappa didn't say anything in response, Annaji said, 'I am going to talk about Marx's theory of history.'

'At the Rotary Club?' asked Krishnappa sarcastically.

'Why not?' Annaji said, also sarcastically. 'Planting the seeds is the job of people like me. Now, take Uma. Hailing from a bureaucrat background, she has come to join the comprador capitalist class. But she is potentially a revolutionist. The rich try to own someone like her as if she were a possession. But...'

'Haven't you become their possession yourself?' Krishnappa said, looking around at the objects of luxury in the room. Annaji brushed aside Krishnappa's comment with an ironic laugh.

Krishnappa sensed that Uma didn't like his staying too long. So he drained his coffee and got up. Annaji urged him to stay, but Krishnappa excused himself saying that he would be at the talk in the evening, and went out and walked towards the hill outside town. He needed to be alone. It was also necessary to stay away from Gowri's house.

* * *

The hill outside town had a cave. A hermit, an old man with a long beard, naked except for a piece of cloth covering his crotch, lived in that cave. Nobody knew his name. He didn't talk to anybody. He would come down the hill every morning, pick a street every day, and standing at one end of the street, he would loudly chant verses from the Bhagavad Gita for an hour. Passers-by would drop rice or pulses or fruits into a basket on the ground. Once the little basket was full, the hermit would accept nothing more. He would return to the hill, cook what had been given, and eat just that.

Krishnappa was curious about this hermit. He went up the hill and sat down on a rock near the cave. The hermit had built a fire outside the cave on which he was cooking the usual rice and dal in an earthen vessel placed on three stones. 'Namaskara,' Krishnappa greeted him. The hermit didn't talk. When the food was cooked, the hermit went into the cave, brought out a few muttuga leaves, and knitting them together with twigs, made three leaf plates. He served the food from the vessel in three equal portions, and placed one plate at a short distance. Krishnappa saw a dog appear from behind some rocks and walk slowly towards the food. The hermit placed the second plate in front of Krishnappa, and sitting down before the last one, meditated with closed eyes. Krishnappa was at a loss, so once the hermit started eating, he ate what was before him without a word. The food had no taste, but he was hungry, he ate.

When he had finished eating, the hermit went away to discard the leaf plate at a distance. Krishnappa also threw away his plate and returned to where they were sitting. Even then, the hermit didn't talk. After a while, Krishnappa didn't feel the need to talk either. The hermit lay down in the shade and closed his eyes. Is this hermit a fake or genuine? A liberated soul or an idiot? – such questions seemed irrelevant. It made Krishnappa still more bewildered. I must be feeling this way because of the many possibilities confronting me, he thought. I could roll off these boulders and die. Or like this hermit, eat one meal a day and live quietly. Or engage in conflict with society, like Annaji. Or sleep with Gowri every night, make love to her, and beget children. No need to do anything. Or any of those things could be done. Or nothing at all, like now. Even then, that's doing something. Nothing can have meaning. And if it does, it is what one gives it.

The hermit woke up. There was an impassive look on his face. He got up, disappeared behind a boulder and urinated. He came back and slept.

Does this hermit start his day with a decision to be like this? Or has his decision already been made? Is he happy? Does it even matter to him?

He will be like this until tomorrow, won't he? Every day, he declaims, 'Do your duty, do it without expectation. Neither dwell, nor despair,' and so on from the Gita, and earns his day's meal. What keeps him going? Nagged by such questions, Krishnappa sprang to his feet and said suddenly, 'Please, swami! I have a question.' His eyes blinked, but the hermit continued sleeping.

'Have you taken a vow of silence? Then why do you sing the Bhagavad Gita in the streets every day? What is your purpose?'

The hermit didn't turn his head. He may be deaf, Krishnappa thought. He realized that his speaking to the hermit meant little more than screaming at nobody. But he couldn't bear it any more. He went and sat near the hermit, and shouted, 'Say something!'

He had become utterly absurd. Feeling helpless, he grasped the hermit's hand tightly. Without protest, the hermit let his hand remain there and stared towards the east. Krishnappa felt like screaming. The eyes, the ears, the nose, the touch, all constantly bring the outside into one's inside. The penis and the vagina join the inside and the outside all the more intimately, don't they? What truth other than this could the ascetic have discovered? Isn't it because I expected a reaction from him that his mysteriousness has become more of an enigma to me? He could be an idiot, but he has triumphed over me. I should get him to react, even if I have to force him – Krishnappa felt tempted for a moment, but resisted. Frustrated, he stood up, and dragging heavy feet, went down the hill, towards the town.

Krishnappa marvelled at how Annaji sat through the rituals of the Rotary Club meeting. He watched Annaji as he spoke, in fluent English, about the intimate connection between the individual and society, about the need for change in the means of production, about class consciousness and revolution. He felt disgust at how the audience, dressed in their silk jubbas and suits, was enjoying the speech, in English, on revolution, as though it were a lullaby. Like karma and rebirth, revolution was also inevitable from time to time, not different from an epoch-ending apocalypse. Why not, Krishnappa thought. Channaveerayya was beaming with satisfaction. Before the vote of thanks, Krishnappa got up and left for the hostel.

* * *

It was dark. Gowri Deshpande's car stood in front of the hostel. The driver was smoking outside the car. The boys of the hostel stood in clusters, talking animatedly among themselves. It was the first time that a female creature of any kind had entered the hostel. The boys didn't expect so much as a female insect in their midst. Gowri Deshpande's visit had become a historical event. They stopped buzzing when they saw Krishnappa. He went up the stairs and opened the door to his room. Gowri, who was absorbed in a book, stood up.

'Forgive me for coming to your room and bothering you,' she said softly and smiled. Her broad milk-complexioned face looked calm. She wore a large dot of kumkum on her forehead. On the one hand, her full lower lip, her heavy breasts, the fullness of her limbs, the arched posture of her body, the dark, sumptuous braid that fell on her back – they made her enticing. But her big, tranquil eyes and finely curved eyebrows made him feel that she was unattainable. She seemed to him a mysterious mermaid hiding deep in silent waters. With unconcealed joy at finding her there, Krishnappa stood before her like a sculpture carved from black stone.

'May I sit?' Gowri asked with a mischievous smile. As there was just one chair, she looked around for a place. Krishnappa sat on the bed and gestured towards the chair. Gowri noticed the pictures on the wall, of Vivekananda and Gandhiji whom Krishnappa venerated.

'Is it true that you are dropping out of college?' she asked.

'Yes, because I want to do something else. Not because of you.'

Krishnappa understood that Gowri was relieved. She said:

'I got your letter. Except my mother, the only one I have is you. Is it respect? Is it love? How to tell? But please don't mind that I said this to you in so many words. I had no real reason for coming here.'

Gowri had spoken quite normally. Krishnappa, who sat with his head bowed, said:

'You have come here alone, to the boys' hostel. What will your mother say?'

'I never thought that you too would ask such a question…' Noticing the embarrassment her answer had caused Krishnappa, she smiled and added, 'My mother left my father after he went to jail. She does not come in the way of my wishes.'

'Hope you are not here out of spite?' said Krishnappa, having recovered himself.

'Why do you think it's spite? I told you that I like you. But you are conceited, aren't you? You didn't expect that I would say such things either, because that's how you are by nature.'

Krishnappa was perplexed. Gowri got up and saying, 'Come home when you feel like,' she left.

Krishnappa has come to realize that as love becomes intense, the object of love seems to become unattainable. What we desire intensely, we don't get to enjoy. Or when desire becomes intense, there is no enjoyment, Krishnappa says to himself as he lies facing death.

Love, desire, frustration – thus Gowri had stuck him in an inexorable wheel of fire. After spending yet another sleepless night, Krishnappa went to see Annaji in the morning. Having finished with breakfast, Annaji was sitting in the garden with Channaveerayya. In his broken English, Channaveerayya was telling him how much his friends had liked the speech, how even the big-shot advocates were impressed with his English. He kept looking up at Krishnappa, puzzling over his status, unable to decide whether to offer him a chair or whether he was to be left standing the whole time he was there, when he saw Annaji get up eagerly to offer his own. 'Don't, I'll get him another chair,' Channaveerayya said, and shouted loudly, 'Ye Maada, ye Maada, where did you go?' With Annaji standing, he too got to his feet. He looked up and down at Krishnappa who, it seemed, was worthy of Annaji's respect.

'This is Mr Krishnappa Gowda. In ten years' time, he will be a great leader of this country – a leader of the farmers. He is someone given to original thinking, capable of carrying out grassroots politics,' said Annaji, introducing Krishnappa. Channaveerayya looked down at the grass on the lawn, giving Annaji cause to enjoin on him this English lesson:

'Grassroots – it's an idiom. For example, Gandhi's politics is grassroots politics. Not aiming at superficial change only, but trying to change the conscience of the common people. That was the subject of my talk yesterday.'

Channaveerayya said, meaning to include Krishnappa in the conversation, 'The standard of English has gone down so much these days, even double graduates don't know it well. Isn't it so, Mr Krishnappa? If any Tom, Dick and Harry is made a teacher in the name of democracy, how can our children be expected to learn?'

Krishnappa had come here to see Annaji in order to avoid going to Gowri Deshpande's house. But he couldn't stand the buffoonery that was being enacted on the lawn.

'Excuse me, I have to go,' he said. But then Uma appeared bearing a coffee tray and he sat down, as if on needles, to drink the brew. When he was ready to leave, Channaveerayya had gone off to tell the driver to bring the car around. Krishnappa went up with Annaji to his room above the garage. Closing the door, he said, 'Annaji, I dropped out of college. I'm fed up with playing a children's game.'

In his joy, Annaji made to hug Krishnappa. Seeing him shrink away, he remembered his uneasiness about bodies touching, and let his outstretched hands drop.

'Great! Go to the villages then!' he said, lighting a cigarette. They sat in silence for some time.

'Even the DSP had come to the meeting yesterday,' said Krishnappa, looking at Annaji's face questioningly.

'Yes, I'm trying to be respectable. But look at this,' he said, getting up to show a column published in an inside page of that day's *Hindu* newspaper. It was about a man who called himself Swamiji, a fugitive wanted by the police for provoking violence among the farmers of the Telangana region. There was a reward. It included a description of the man as having a shaved head, wearing an ochre-coloured jubba and dhoti, of tall stature and a face with sharp features. Krishnappa looked in suspicion at Annaji, who looked like a Bengali gentleman, when Annaji went and took out from his trunk an ochre-coloured jubba and dhoti. He wrapped it in paper and said, 'No more use for this. Burn it.'

'And then?' said Krishnappa.

'When you return to your village, hide me somewhere. Right now, I'll keep my identity secret by writing critically of Marxism from the perspective of M.N. Roy. You'll see.' He pointed to the photos of Lincoln and Roosevelt which he had clipped from one of his books and displayed on the wall.

Krishnappa had wanted to tell him about his inexplicable anxieties, but now didn't feel like making the effort. He wrapped the ochre garments in that day's *Hindu,* and as he got up to leave there was a knock on the door. Annaji's eyes lit up with joy.

Saying, 'It must be Uma. Marvellous woman. Every revolutionary should have a woman like her by his side,' he went to the door.

'May I come in?' Uma said, a book of Gorky's short stories in hand.

'Stay, we are going to discuss Gorky,' Annaji said to Krishnappa. But Krishnappa didn't want to stay. Observing how Uma's eyes gleamed with love, how her ample breasts rose and fell with her breath, stirred an uncomfortable jealousy in him. Annaji might have been self-conscious about being alone with her. Urging him to stay, but perhaps only for form, he walked down the stairs with Krishnappa and said goodbye.

Drawn by desire, Krishnappa walked towards Gowri's house. Near her house, he became uneasy. At the gate of her house, he hoped that she wouldn't be home. Seeing no car in the portico, he felt his anxiety ebb. He had forgotten that she would have gone to college at this time. But then, her mother might have taken the car too. A servant who was working in the garden noticed him.

'Little Madam is not home. Do you want to see Big Madam?' Krishnappa said no and walked away quickly. He felt relieved.

He wandered aimlessly for some time. As the day grew warmer, he started up the hill, having resolved to himself: today I am going to crack the code of that hermit's silence. He hadn't eaten breakfast in the morning, hadn't slept all night. He was hungry and fatigued.

Already from a distance he had seen the hermit making the fire for a meal. It had made Krishnappa hungrier. He sat leaning against a boulder like the previous day. The hermit placed a pot on the fire, brought out a thick book from the cave, and sat down to read. If he got up to look at what it was, Krishnappa feared the hermit's concentration would break, so he remained where he was. After a while, the hermit fetched muttuga leaves and knitted three plates from them. I am being included, to that extent he has acknowledged my existence, he thought. The dog appeared from some corner and made for the shadow of a boulder, where it lay panting with its tongue hanging out. A grey-coloured dog with black spots, it must have followed this hermit some time and camped out here.

When the food in the pot was cooked and the hermit began portioning it out into three parts, Krishnappa went closer. The hermit was placing the dog's meal and Krishnappa saw what he was reading – the Valmiki Ramayana in Sanskrit. They ate in silence. Today, in addition to rice and dal, there was coconut and sweet jaggery. Someone must have put them in the hermit's begging bowl.

Krishnappa wanted to make conversation with the hermit. What if I asked him about the question that has been bothering me the most, he thought.

'Sometimes I don't know what to do. I am confronted with hundreds of possibilities. Why should one go on living? I'm not sure.'

The hermit sat eating, betraying no emotion, as if Krishnappa should know that his was an absurd cry. He pondered his question, whether it was a wrong or concocted one, or whether he was stupid to be confessing his inner thoughts to some fool. He got up without finishing the food, threw away the leaf, went and washed his hands in a nearby stream. When he came back, he witnessed an event which made the hermit even more mysterious to him.

An old man, wearing a topi and a cotton cloth wrapped over his shirt, stood in front of the hermit who was eating. Wiping the sweat off his face with the cloth, he asked for water. The hermit pointed towards the water and the leaf cup. The old man drank from the cup, splashed his eyes, and asked, 'I have to get to the Mookambika temple, but I've lost my way. Is it very far from here?'

The hermit had finished eating. He got up, washed his hands, came back, and said, 'Go this way, turn right at that big boulder. There are steps there. Climb about a hundred steps, and you'll find the temple.'

When the old man left after respectfully thanking him with joined palms, Krishnappa looked at the hermit with surprise and asked, 'How is it that you don't talk to me?'

There was no answer. Now, as he goes through the physical exercises to get the circulation going in his stricken left side, Krishnappa remembers the incident and says:

'The hermit would answer only if the question was factual. He would not answer those questions that were about opinions. Whereas Annaji was a man who was by nature expansive, the hermit opened himself to the world only as far as it was necessary. Whether this achieved inner ripeness for him, whether he or anyone else gained anything from it, is hard to say. For that matter, I or Annaji – what did we accomplish in the end?'

When he gets this way, Krishnappa is usually very sad. So it cannot conclusively be said to reflect the totality of his views. This much is true – the hermit had got to him. The desire to become silent like the hermit and let the inner fire blaze hasn't left him even now – not even when he is losing control over his excretory functions.

Once Krishnappa saw that the hermit did speak after all, he tried hard to search for a question that would make him respond. The question had to be real and clear-cut, like 'which way to such and such place'. But he feared that all his troubles might be rooted in the yearnings of his mind, or perhaps he didn't really know what his troubles were. Even if a question were possible, he thought, it might be beyond the hermit's grasp. Or the hermit might be of the view that no one could solve someone else's problem.

As evening fell, Krishnappa came down the hill. He wondered whether he should go to Gowri's. But then, what would he say to her? Surely he was acting immaturely, he felt, and turned towards his hostel. The boys there appeared eager to ask him something. He was tired and told them that they could talk the next day. He went to his room to go to bed. He drank the milk that Kishorekumar had brought up for him, and opening the envelope the boy had brought along, read eagerly:

> It must have been you who came to my house asking for me earlier today. Mother, who was upstairs, told me it was someone who looked like a poet. Who else could it be but you? Come tomorrow – that is, if you feel like. Please don't hesitate. Yours – Gowri Deshpande.

A happiness came upon Krishnappa. And a fright, too.

These days, as he lies fighting with death, he reflects on what went on in those days and wonders. How is it that we are more fascinated by the woman whom our love cannot have than the woman our love has won over? Why wasn't it possible for him to tell her straight away that he desired her? Why was it that even she, who could talk so freely, jovially, intelligently, couldn't suggest, in the way a woman who wants a man does, that she too wanted him? As he imagined her goddess's face, it was not possible for him to desire her shapely body. Whenever he longed for her body, he would remember her face, the way she talked, the way she looked, and would be left feeling disgust for his desires. So in those days, it was impossible for him to articulate all that he felt for her – that he desired her with his whole being – in the form of a single utterance, a question, or a firm conviction.

Krishnappa slept well that night. Until, in the middle of the night, he was woken up by some commotion. He turned the light on. As he went down the stairs, he saw that the hostel boys were excitedly dragging someone in. Krishnappa hurried down, but Shamanna pushed him back into his room, closed the door behind them, and joined his palms. He appeared drunk, and was panting and babbling.

'Right now, please don't say anything. We will ask you to come down, but only once we have made those brahmin boys spit up their sambar-saaru. We'll make them fall at your feet. But I swear, we won't harm them,' Shamanna said, and scurrying out of the room, he bolted the door. There was nothing Krishnappa could do as the ruckus grew outside the door. The boys, some of them normally shy, were shouting abuses. *Dhub, dhub,* the sounds of people being punched and pummelled. A shouting match. And then, everything was quiet. The door was unlatched. Shamanna came in and said:

'If you want, take us all to task tomorrow, but now please come down. Those pigs have agreed to apologize to you.'

Krishnappa went down and saw: it was pandemonium. Ramu, the gang leader, was tied to the leg of a cot. His face was smeared with ashes from the hostel's kitchen fire. Two of his companions had their hands tied and their legs secured to the window's bars with a rope. Ramu's ash-smeared face, with its whiskers, was grotesque from fear, anger and humiliation. Shamanna stood before him, and gloating in his triumph, started conducting a trial in Krishnappa's presence – addressing Ramu in the respectful form. But Krishnappa was not unaware that, prior to the present stage of the operation, the culprits had been subjected to whatever means could be employed.

'Did you write those filthy things on the wall of our hostel in the middle of the night?'

'Hmm ...' Ramu replied in a surly tone.

'Do you admit that what you did was like eating shit?'

Seeing Shamanna pull out a bicycle chain from his trouser pocket, Ramu grimaced.

'Yes ...' he said.

'Mr Krishnappa Gowda is a leader to all of us here. You must apologize to him. But before you do, we will set you free, because your apology must be voluntary and genuine.'

Krishnappa was surprised to see this side of Shamanna, whom he had thought of as a dandy. The boys took their cue from Shamanna and freed all three. Ramu, who stood stiffly, turned to Krishnappa and said:

'They had us remove our watches and give them over. Ask them to return them.'

'Look, we are not thieves,' said Shamanna and returned the three watches. All of them stood in a circle to surround the three boys who were made to face Krishnappa.

Krishnappa told them in his calm and unruffled voice:

'I don't want an apology from you. You think that we – I and Gowri Deshpande – are your kind, and so you do things like this, which is not right. What can you do, you poor chaps? You and I are in college, both wasting our time, and you get the mistaken idea that I am like you.'

Ramu turned to leave, but he was stopped by Shamanna, who glowered at him and said, 'He may not want it. But we demand that you apologize.'

'Sorry. Please forgive,' Ramu mumbled.

'Bring me a bucket of water,' Shamanna ordered his boys. When the bucket was brought, he dipped a towel in the water and approached Ramu to wipe his face. Ramu looked away to avert this.

'You see, now that you have apologized, it is my duty to wipe away the ash I smeared on your face,' Shamanna said.

Ramu didn't let him. He wiped it himself. Then, Shamanna said, 'Now you must clean the walls. That is the condition.'

Ramu left with his cohort. The hostel stood and watched them wipe away the writings.

In treating the punishment of Ramu and his companions as a cheap victory, Krishnappa thought he had taken the high road. But he now feels that he might have even wanted them punished. Later in his political career, on many an occasion, his indifference became a weapon for destroying his adversaries. Without his asking, others have carried out what needed doing. Is it right to get others to do the dirty work while keeping pure? He has wondered about this. But in those days, subtle ethical questions were trivial before the quest for social justice. Didn't Annaji say that once you have firmly committed to the fight of the oppressed, whatever your means, they are just? The beliefs that gave him a headstrong personality are proving to be troublesome for Krishnappa who, at this moment, is learning to fold and unfold his fingers, one at a time. You might have lived solely for the welfare of others, but there is no certainty that you have remained whole.

On the following morning, Krishnappa went to see Gowri Deshpande. She hadn't gone to college and was home that day. Her mother Anasuyabayi appeared pleased that her daughter had, at last, come to like some young man. A slim, tall-looking woman, she came down the stairs in a green silk sari and played the host unobtrusively. Though her hair showed a few strands of white, her face retained its youthful liveliness and charm. She placed before Krishnappa and her daughter some snacks to eat and coffee in a flask, told them to carry on with their conversation, and went to her room.

Gowri offered to serve uppittu to Krishnappa, trying to loosen him up.

'What are your plans for the future?'

She noticed that Krishnappa was finding it difficult to answer.

'Don't know. I'll go back to my village. I have a mother ... a small piece of land. I'll do whatever comes to mind once I start living there. What about you?'

Krishnappa wouldn't have asked it merely as courtesy. When he finished eating uppittu, Gowri cut an apple for him. Mr Nanjappa had ordered a basket of apples from Shimla for her mother, she told him, and trying to hide her wish to see his reaction, asked:

'Do you think it's all right that a girl may not have the desire to become a mother?'

Krishnappa hadn't expected a question like that. Gowri waited patiently.

'I haven't thought about it. I thought it was natural for a woman to want children.'

'It's not that. What I'm saying is that she may love children, but may not want to be a mother.'

'Why? Out of fear?'

'No. Not even out of fear. A woman may want a man for intimacy, but may not want to be an instrument for begetting children. Do you think it is abnormal?'

'If I felt that way, I would try to understand why I feel that way. But if you are asking me in a general way, I don't know what to say.'

'Come, let's sit in that room and talk,' Gowri said eagerly.

She put a box of Players before him and said, 'You may smoke, if you want.' Nanjappa might have had them there for himself, Krishnappa thought. He lit a cigarette, and listened to Gowri:

'Yes, I feel that way. But don't think it is because of the unusual circumstances I am in. Though Mother thinks so, and it makes her very unhappy. You see, I want to travel to other parts of the world, read widely, meet a variety of people – I feel like doing many things. I don't want to be tied to a man and be living all my life as his wife.'

Krishnappa was silent. Gowri said, with a laugh, 'You must be shocked, right? But I really feel that way. Moreover, I'm a little bit like my mother – I need a man. I also believe that I am not a flirt. Come, let's go.'

To make it unnecessary for him to answer, Gowri took Krishnappa to the garden outside and showed him the roses. She showed him a nest some bird had made in the trunk of a tree in one corner. Pointing to an infant bird nestled in soft feathers that was crying *chi chi* with its pink mouth open, Gowri pressed her face against his arm quite naturally. Krishnappa felt that she had lost herself in a moment of happiness. When he was a young boy, he used to go looking for nests. Sometimes he shot the birds with his slingshot and hurt them. But today, Gowri's rapture made him soft too. Dressed in a crisply ironed white sari with a floral design, her braid falling on her chest, she turned her face to Krishnappa. Her eyes were moist with joy. Krishnappa patted her gently, but checked himself against wanting to press her closer to him.

He proposed an excursion to the hill. 'Shall we go in the car?' she said. He hesitated but agreed, for that distance on foot may have tired her. On the way, he told her about Maheshwarayya and Annaji. He surprised himself, talking so freely. When the car stopped at the bottom of the hill, he asked her whether she knew anything of the hermit. She didn't, because she lived outside town.

'Come, let's meet him,' Krishnappa said, as they started up the hill. 'Look, I don't know the answer to your question. It's fine if you feel the way you do. But…'

He saw her breathing hard, and waited. Further on, there was a rock which they had to climb. Gowri tucked up her sari and said easily:

'Please don't think, like my mother does, that I say such things out of spite.'

'No,' said Krishnappa, going up the rock and holding his hand out to her. Gripping his powerful arm, she sprang lightly on to the rock.

'I find politics boring,' she said, as if it was her definitive view. 'I feel that this place is too small. In a big city, you have privacy. That's why I want to go to Bombay or Delhi to study. I don't know how you can live in a village.' Krishnappa searched for her meaning beyond her words.

Outside the hermit's cave, the dog was barking. The hermit, who was bent over the fire, cooking his meal, stood up to calm the dog. When they got to the cave, Gowri, in fright, let out a shriek and clung to Krishnappa. A hooded cobra had frightened the dog as it moved towards the cave. The hermit held the dog back, and the cobra slid into the darkness. The hermit patted the dog and coaxed it away from the cave. In time, the dog grew calmer and lay down in its place, growling and looking at the cave. When the pot of food was done, the hermit walked to the cave to bring out muttuga leaves for the plates. Seeing him prepare to go in, Gowri became frightened, and shaking, she held Krishnappa tightly. A hissing sound came from within. The hermit stood still. The dog had been lying down with its ears pricked, and now it ran up and barked again. The hermit hugged it to himself. He dragged the dog to Krishnappa, and with his eyes, signalled to him to keep the dog. While Krishnappa held the dog, the hermit washed four small spots on the flat surface of a boulder clean with water from the pot. Krishnappa told him that they wouldn't eat, so he served a half portion of the food and placed the rest farther away for the dog. The dog wouldn't eat and ran back to the mouth of the cave and started barking. The hissing continued. The hermit tried once more to drag the dog to its food.

Gowri watched the drama in awe. The dog squirmed in the hermit's arms.

'I thought you were the sort of person who would leave the dog alone,' said Krishnappa, remembering the line from the Gita: *It does not kill, nor is It killed*. Wasn't this from the book he read every day? The hermit appeared to give some serious attention to what Krishnappa said. He sighed softly, and Krishnappa waited curiously for his reaction. The hermit released the dog, which sprang to its feet and stood barking outside the cave. A rising and falling sound filled the cave, as if the cave itself were hissing. Krishnappa saw that the hermit's face had turned pale. Gowri clung to Krishnappa and hid her face in his chest. Krishnappa waited for the inevitable. The dog went into the cave. The cobra's hissing, which could be still heard, gradually became muffled and turned into the sound of a washerman beating his clothes on a stone. A moment later, the dog emerged with the cobra still wriggling in its blood-smeared mouth and ran into the bushes. A trail of blood left the cave, seeing which the hermit scooped up the food he had served himself, threw it away, and came back. It seemed like he was trying to compose himself.

Even now, when he remembers it, Krishnappa wonders whether the hermit ever came to terms with the violence in the incident he had witnessed.

* * *

Krishnappa tries to make progress, first with the right hand, folding and unfolding his fingers gradually. One morning, his elbow and leg come back, which makes him a little hopeful. He thinks of dictating a letter for Gowri Deshpande. She has been teaching English at Miranda House college in Delhi since she came back from America. He will ask her to come see him for a few days. It's been more than fifteen years since he last saw her. She has remained unmarried and without any children. She had written to him from Philadelphia when she was studying there. She had been living in with an American man. Three years of living together, and she realized that he wanted children. He hadn't said as much to her, but she didn't want him to harbour false hopes, and so, she was going to end the relationship. Krishnappa saw that he had been wrong earlier in supposing immaturity to be the reason for her not wanting to have children.

After all, they were anxious times for him. In those days, he felt as if he were tiptoeing along the edge of a bottomless precipice. In his company, Gowri had tried to remain light-hearted and cheerful, but had failed. When they were together, they burned each other out like the piercing flame of a lamp, rather than melting in each other's warmth. She would solicit his attention with something like:

'I haven't told you, have I? When my father was in Belgaum, Nanjappa and he were friends. They were partners in business. Nanjappa used to stay over. It seems my father had another mistress...'

Krishnappa would find such stuff irrelevant and become indifferent to what she was saying. Gowri would feel bad that she was pulling Krishnappa down to trivial matters, whereas he had come to her with lofty expectations. All she could do for him was to make the kinds of things he liked to eat and feed him.

Krishnappa, who visited her every day, would say to her as if she were a stranger:

'Excuse me. You probably want to study. The exams are approaching, aren't they?' She even liked the way he could remain distant while being familiar.

'Not at all. Come,' she would say. Krishnappa would sit in silence, his big eyes roving idly over the room.

'Would you like me to sing?' Gowri would ask to loosen him up. Anasuyabayi would come down the stairs and sit with them, listening to her daughter sing in front of Krishnappa. Krishnappa liked that she came in quietly and took a corner, being a bother to no one. Seeing them together – curly-haired, dark, hard-bodied, statue-like Krishnappa with her milk-complexioned, keenly sensitive daughter – filled Anasuyabayi's heart with joy. They were characters from Sharat Chandra, her favourite novelist. If, sometimes, Nanjappa walked in in the middle of the singing, no one minded. Nanjappa hadn't liked the idea of a poor man like Krishnappa. But he held his tongue as he was afraid of Gowri. He had become devout lately, and after coming back in the evening from the puja at the Ganesha temple, he would hand out the kumkum to all three before taking himself upstairs. Unnoticed by Gowri or Krishnappa, Anasuyabayi too would have got up and left.

Why didn't I sleep with her then, Krishnappa wonders. When he was alone, he desperately wanted to make love to her. But the thought of copulating on all fours, like an animal, would fill him with revulsion. The one who freed him from this guilt was Lucina – Lucina, who shed him of inhibitions and showed him that every bend and nook of the body could come alive. If only it had been with Gowri first…

One afternoon, Krishnappa went to see Annaji. Annaji was no longer scrounging for money. He had more than enough, and he had repaid the loans Krishnappa had managed for him. Krishnappa didn't ask where he got all that money, but Annaji had praised Uma's generosity. She might have been stealing her husband's black money from the safe and passing it on, Krishnappa thought. The impropriety of it wouldn't bother Annaji. His passion for discussing the intricate issues of Marxism and Leninism was undiminished. Uma would be seated attentively with her oil-dark face cupped in her hands. He would keep turning to her as he presented the knottiest arguments. It seemed to Krishnappa that Annaji presented idea after idea to Uma like a worshipper before a goddess, offering flowers at the idol.

That afternoon, as he stood outside the door, Krishnappa heard what sounded like Uma moaning and Annaji whispering to her. He was about to knock on the door, but held back. They must have heard his footsteps, though. Krishnappa could hear their panic-stricken bustling and felt awkward. Should he stand there? Or leave? Neither would be right. In his incertitude, he said, 'It's Krishnappa. I was just passing by. I'll come back another time.'

'Oh! It's Krishnappa! Wait, don't leave.' Annaji sounded greatly relieved.

Krishnappa felt acutely discomfited. He couldn't leave now. He would have to regard Annaji and Uma as if nothing had happened. To make it less difficult for them to pretend, he would have to act stupid, as if he had no idea.

The door opened. Uma was standing on a stool, her hair a mess, dusting the books on the shelves with a cloth. Krishnappa was supposed to think that she couldn't answer the door because she was in the middle of something. But Annaji, rubbing his eyes as if he had just woken up, looked absolutely ludicrous. And yet, within a minute, he was engrossed in the contradictions in Lenin's idea of 'democratic centralism'. Trying to recall a statement of Lenin accurately, Annaji said, 'Uma, get me the *Collected Works* of Lenin, please.' Uma brought him the book.

'She has picked up quicker than Channaveerayya. Also, she is capable of thinking,' Annaji commented, as he searched the book for the passage he had in mind. Uma went downstairs to bring coffee.

Krishnappa felt an intense jealousy for the first time in his life that day. He noticed a blissful languor in her walk. Why can't I be like Annaji? he thought, feeling intensely discontented. If a man like Annaji, whose body doesn't seem to hunger or thirst, could so easily take his fulfilment from a woman, why not I? I can't so much as fantasize about Gowri being naked. The jealousy that swept through him that day remained with Krishnappa long after Annaji died. He lost it later, when Lucina, caressing him with her lips and the tip of her tongue, turned his body into a flaming bed and offered it her own leopard-like body. When Krishnappa got up to leave, Annaji said without a trace of embarrassment:

'Don't go. Sit. Otherwise Uma might become suspicious that you have come to know. What you guessed is right. But I have no control over these things.'

Krishnappa was amazed that Annaji could be so casual in this situation.

* * *

Krishnappa was even more amazed that Uma – wrapped modestly in her sari, a large dot of kumkum on her forehead, her nose pierced with an ornament of precious stone, everything that proclaimed her a married woman – stood demurely, holding coffee in her hands. Is one to think that a woman also can break social boundaries and not suffer from guilt, Krishnappa wondered. His voice full of affection, Annaji said, 'Come, Uma. Sit. I want to talk to you both about a serious matter.' When she sat down, he began in his unique manner of lecturing to a class:

'All the rules relating to production which society has created until now limit the freedom of human beings. Let's take the man–woman relationship. Like other commodities, the woman is also treated as property. Thus, in both feudal and capitalist societies, man has devised a system of protecting a woman as his property by creating two categories – a woman who is one's own, and a woman who is someone else's. All such systems hamper the natural development of human beings. As a result, this libido – our sexuality – has become subjected to unnatural restrictions. The capitalist system rests on scarcity – artificially created scarcity and exploitation. This applies to our sex lives as well. You see, as man's need for food, clothing and shelter, and his cultural needs come to be satisfied through prosperity, he becomes ready for his ultimate liberation. Then, tearing down all those restrictions on sexuality that have subjected them to pain and suffering, men and women will become liberated. Those restrictions that limit sexual pleasure to married couples only, or to certain kinds of permissible pleasures of the body, will disappear then. As the ownership of property disappears in the classless society, the body too becomes liberated and becomes a fount of joy. The attainment of that joy brings a sense of morality to man. Can there be any morality greater than cherishing what we enjoy as most valuable and free?'

'Can't your argument be seen as your justification for your lifestyle?' Krishnappa said bitterly, neglecting for a moment to account for Uma's presence in the room.

'Forget my situation. But think, Krishnappa. You are from a community of farmers. Your forefathers were landowners. Therefore, you are basically feudal in matters of women,' Annaji ventured this half in jest.

'If it's feudal to believe that one should not live an unprincipled life, or to think of women as sacred, then so be it.'

'Tell me, why is a woman sacred? Because she is someone's property. Those who say she is sacred are themselves wifebeaters, who think women are good only for cooking, for singing, and as ornaments. They regard the women who are willing to sleep with them as trash…'

The last statement stung Krishnappa because it touched him in a deeply personal way. It is true, he thought, that Uma was here with Annaji right now as if she were an untainted woman. But at night, she would have to offer her body to her husband too, wouldn't she? Would her body become a fount of pleasure under the attentions of the gold-toothed Channaveerayya, as it did with Annaji? How else would she offer herself? Krishnappa's nature on the whole was opposed to the thought of two men sharing a woman. Perhaps Uma went through the act mechanically with her husband, and blossomed really for Annaji. In that case, she should leave her husband. It could have been argued about with Annaji if Uma wasn't present, Krishnappa thought as he bit back his words.

It was still on his mind that evening when he went to see Gowri. Yes, he wanted her, but she was not someone who would move with him to the village. To ask her to sleep with him without marrying her would be to treat her as an object of pleasure. Even if she were willing, he was sure he would think of her as trash afterwards. Battling within himself thus, he answered Gowri's questions with 'huh's and soon left. The next day, he went to the hermit. The hermit was reading the same book as before. Why would I ask this man, Krishnappa thought, feeling weary. When the hermit started cooking, he got up to leave. Perhaps the hermit would have liked to ask him to stay on, but his vows were in the way. Krishnappa sensed the hesitation in the expression on the hermit's face. Such forced self-denial, he told himself on his way down the hill, was not his way of living.

Now, he is in his wheelchair, being pushed around by his wife, and Krishnappa thinks: Here I am. I was thinking of hitting my wife.

I have lived my life single-mindedly for a cause. Having failed even there, I've dried up. I am dying a slow death. No one comes to me to talk about their love lives. Those who come only bring news of people who have defected from the party or are about to defect. How did I get to be like this?

I have all these thoughts dogging me because of the state of my body, he thinks angrily.

'Ye, Nagesha!' he shouts. Nagesh, who is the secretary of the party's youth wing, presents himself and asks, 'What is it, Gowdre?'

'Don't you have a girlfriend with whom you are in love, that sort of thing?' Krishnappa laughs.

'Who, me? Where do I have time for that, Gowdre? With all these problems facing the country…' Nagesh says in his serious, humourless manner.

'That's all right. Now take down this statement I want to make.' Krishnappa starts dictating the statement, a statement that will scare other politicians, a statement he must make that very day.

Nagesh takes it down excitedly. With affection and amusement, Krishnappa looks at his handsome face with its trace of a moustache and beard and his shoulder-length hair. At his age, hadn't Krishnappa plunged into politics to show the world that he was a man, a somebody? He tells himself that he will send for Gowri Deshpande tomorrow. Wouldn't she have come on her own if she still cared for him? She lives in Delhi with her mother, he has been told. Every day, he thinks of sending for her, but feeling self-conscious about his condition, he puts it off.

Now, when he might die, he is haunted by the question of whether he has kept his integrity.

* * *

On his wheelchair, Krishnappa has a vision of a parade of men: the administrator of a mutth, Narasimha Bhatta, whom he hated intensely; a prominent betel-nut planter, Shivananja Gowda; Veerabhadrappa who, as a PWD minister, took lakhs in bribes and became the chief minister of the state; and that fat-faced police officer from Warangal. Attacking them are frenzied women with scraggly hair, carrying spindle-legged children in their arms, and peasants in their faded, short dhotis. Torturing them a little at a time, they kill them slowly. They bring the blood of their victims to rub on his paralysed leg and side. Someone shouts, 'Hey, this blood won't do. What he needs is the warm blood of a pigeon!' Krishnappa laughs.

Just then, Gowri comes in to tell him something, but seeing her father staring ahead ferociously as if in a trance, she is scared of him. Krishnappa thinks that he can move his leg and tries to lift it by concentrating his mind entirely on his foot. He is confident that he will be able to lift his leg, but all that moves is his toe. Krishnappa lets out a sigh and returns to dreaming. This time, the peasants are not killing. Rather, they have lined up their pot-bellied enemies and are putting them on trial quite seriously.

Part Two

What took him back to his own place to organize the peasant struggle was Annaji's capture and his subsequent murder.

Annaji had begun to look as well-fed and paunchy as the self-satisfied bourgeoisie he ridiculed. Uma knew the whole story of his life. She had told him that she would run away with him wherever he went. He made light of it when he talked about it with Krishnappa. But he was beginning to worry that the craze for English would leave Channaveerayya and be replaced by the knowledge that Uma was stealing from his safe and carrying on with the tutor besides. They would then be forced to come to a decision together. Krishnappa was impassive as he listened to Annaji hold forth on his antics. He noticed how free Uma was in his presence, now that she was sure of his closeness to Annaji. There was not a trace of remorse – she was just someone who was preparing to run away with her lover. He noted that her passionate attachment had Annaji in an emotional quandary. They couldn't even talk about his favourite subjects without her being present. Krishnappa marvelled at the way Annaji then went about presenting some dry political tract, whether she understood it or not, as if it were the hot topic of love. Uma thought she would work in a village alongside Annaji. Annaji had decided to head to Kerala to open a tutorial school. Uma had started learning a little Malayalam – already enough to get by in the marketplace – from a carpenter who had come from Kerala to work in their house. In two weeks, they would be gone. Uma had packed her most essential clothing in a small trunk that she kept in Annaji's room. Channaveerayya, who only returned home past midnight after evenings of gambling and drinking at the club, was happy that his wife didn't make a fuss, unlike the wives of his friends. He was proud that he had her under his authority.

One afternoon, a police jeep drove up and stopped outside. Annaji was with Uma, talking to her. Hearing a knock, Annaji opened the door without thinking, expecting Krishnappa. Standing before him, looking like a large demon, was the DSP himself. 'You must come with me to the station,' he said to Annaji. An alarmed Uma stood up.

'Don't be afraid, Uma,' Annaji said. 'There must be some misunderstanding. Send Krishnappa to the police station. I may need bail.' To impress the police, he spoke in fluent English as he stepped out with the DSP.

When Krishnappa arrived some time later, Uma began to cry. Krishnappa, who never could bear to see a woman cry, sat confused, not knowing what to say. Uma handed him a thousand rupees to get Annaji released somehow. At the police station, he heard that Annaji was being taken in a jeep directly to Warangal.

'There's a charge of attempted murder against him. Just be careful, mister!' the police inspector warned him. Annaji was going to be brought before the court in Warangal.

Krishnappa went back to see Uma. Channaveerayya had rushed home and was consoling his wife.

'Look, Mr Krishnappa,' Channaveerayya said. 'It seems that in the name of making a revolution, he got himself involved in some killing. He was living an underground life here, they say. Thank god it's all over. But you see, my wife has great regard for him because of his knowledge. If you want to help your friend somehow, please go there, to Warangal. Here, take these five hundred rupees. His fee for the month was due. But please don't involve me. After all, I am a businessman. These things are very delicate.'

Krishnappa took this money as well, and just as he was leaving for the Warangal train, who should turn up? Maheshwarayya!

He said, 'I'll come with you. I know some Telugu as well.'

Maheshwarayya's hair was longer and greyer. The freshly glistening kumkum on his forehead marked the recent completion of his ritual prayers before the goddess. He went to buy two first-class train tickets. In town, he paid off the loans Krishnappa had taken on account of Annaji which remained unpaid still. They went to a khadi cloth store, and there Maheshwarayya bought him six finely woven dhotis, lengths of cotton for jubbas, and one piece for a woollen coat, which he ordered stitched, instructing the tailor precisely on how wide the sleeves should be, what the collar should look like, how the jubba should taper, etc. To Krishnappa he said that he should wear his dhoti tucked in the back, in the style of a gentleman.

Alighting in Warangal two days later, they rushed to the police station in a taxi. 'Where have you kept R.L. Naik?' they asked a police officer who didn't so much as ask them to sit down.

'What is he to you?' he asked.

'He is my friend,' said Krishnappa.

'Answer carefully. By what name did he become your friend? What all do you know about him? Was he known to you only as R.L. Naik?'

Before Krishnappa could say more, Maheshwarayya, an experienced man in matters of the world, said:

'We guessed it was his name because you arrested him in that name. In our place, he went by the name of Annaji, and he used to give lessons to this man here as an English tutor.'

'Oh, do you know who he is, young man? That scoundrel, a so-called communist, was training rogues and criminals in the Telangana region to kill the zamindars. Because you are in khadi, I am taking the trouble to warn you: don't admit to anyone that you were acquainted with him. He's finished. See this?' The officer brought out the day's English newspaper.

In the newspaper, printed under a photo of Annaji in his ochre garb, was the heading: 'The Accused in Ochre Dead.' Included in the report was a statement made by the police according to which the accused, who had been hiding out in Karnataka, was being brought in a jeep when a group of his followers ambushed the vehicle in the middle of the jungle. Two policemen were injured in the encounter, and caught in the shower of bullets, R.L. Swami alias Annaji died. The report said that there was a possibility that some of this Swami's followers were hiding in Karnataka, and that the Karnataka police were searching the jungles for them.

Krishnappa's face turned pale as he read the report. He stared at that fat-faced officer who held a stick in his hands.

'Did you read the last bit?' asked the fat-faced officer. 'Be careful. If you say you are acquainted with that son of a bitch, we will have to arrest you as well.'

'You son of a bitch! Murderer! Pig!' Krishnappa lunged at the policeman and grabbed his collar. Two constables came running up and pulled him away.

Maheshwarayya folded his hands before the officer. 'Sir, the young man, very short-tempered. Please let him go,' he said in Telugu.

'No pleading with this dirty fellow. Let's go,' Krishnappa said.

'I'll see what nerve you've got. I'll file a case against you for assault and bring you before the magistrate. Until then, I'll keep you here ... Take this wretched kumkum-dotted priest away. Keep an eye on him and see that he doesn't run off. They're all murderers in disguise,' said the officer, standing up. He straightened his uniform and twirled his moustache.

As he was being pushed out by a constable, Maheshwarayya shouted, 'Don't worry, I'll get you a lawyer. Chant the prayer to the Devi.' And with that, he was gone from the police station.

The police officer presented Krishnappa before a dwarfish, mouse-faced magistrate. He told the magistrate that Krishnappa had tried to assault him, that he was an associate of Mr Swami, and that he should be given into his custody for further questioning. Under the magistrate's seal, the officer took Krishnappa to a different police station in the town. He took him to the backyard, and there he told the policeman who stood guard outside a room to open it. The door opened with a creak.

* * *

It was windowless. A musty smell assailed Krishnappa's nostrils. They pushed him inside, and tossed a coarse rug at his feet. In the light that came through the opened door, the police constable pointed to one rusty bowl meant as a toilet and another rusty bowl for drinking water.

'Just remember, the two vessels are for two different uses,' he said, speaking in Urdu, and laughed.

In Krishnappa's pockets, he found the one thousand and five hundred rupees, cigarettes, matches and a pen, which he handed to the officer.

The Warangal heat was unbearable. The dust inside smothered him. Krishnappa was taking in the cobweb-infested, hot-as-an-oven room in the dim light, when the door closed behind him. It became pitch dark.

Krishnappa spread the rug on the dusty floor and tried it. In the heat, it was unbearable to sit on. But his legs were tired from standing. So he sat on the rug, removed his shirt, and wiped his face and the rest of his body with it. He wanted to smoke a cigarette. The policeman had emptied his pockets, and still he searched, hoping to find something.

The first thought that came to him: I shouldn't lose control over my mind. I mustn't succumb to the unexpected adversity that has swooped down upon me. As much as possible, I must rest and conserve my energy to face what is to come. He lay down on the prickly rug. He was sweating and he was thirsty. He couldn't see the water bowl in the dark. The thought of drinking from it was disgusting.

He tried closing his eyes. If he moved even slightly, the dust would rise and cover his face. He wished he could see at least a ray of light through a corner of the door. But the door, made of one solid piece of wood, was shut tight. If I stay here, I won't know the day from the night, he thought. It was not his first time in a jail. He had been to jail during the '42 Quit India Movement, and then again during the

'47 Mysore Liberation Movement. Going to jail had meant being with friends, singing and eating together. 'When you confront the system itself, then you realize the hierarchical nature of the regime' – in the dark, he remembered Annaji's words. They had killed him as if he were an animal. Annaji, perhaps, had dreamt of settling down with a woman peacefully into family life. As he thought about it, Krishnappa's body burned with anger. Lying on the rug, he fantasized about his dark, supine body uncoiling into a gigantic snake and killing those murderers with its venom, when he felt on his skin sharp pricks in a hundred places. He sat up and rubbed himself with his hand. Something sticky and foul-smelling came off on his fingers, and he realized that the needles upon him were bedbugs. Getting up, he rubbed himself all over. A patch on his back which he could not reach was beset by bedbugs. They were crawling on his neck. He scrubbed them with his shirt.

He didn't know how long he had been there. A scratching sound intensified in a corner. It must be the bowl, he thought. Probably mice are scraping it with their front legs. Yes, there is squeaking from that direction. They must be scratching the bowl for food left over by the previous prisoner, for grains of rice sticking to the bottom. Krishnappa stared in the direction of the sound. The bedbugs had fallen off. He kept up the rubbing so that they wouldn't crawl up his legs. If there were even a little light, perhaps the eyes of the mice would shine back. The mice must have burrowed into the room, there must be tunnels. Krishnappa tried to think of the stories he had read, where he might have come across someone who had to spend nights and days like this in a dark room. He thought of the hero in *The Count of Monte Cristo* who bored a hole in his cell, made it bigger and bigger, and escaped in the end. He tried to remember what tool the hero had used, and how he was able to keep it from the guards, etc.

If there was a tunnel that the mice had made, he could widen it little by little. What tool could he use? Could the bowl be steel? Probably not. If it were, he could fashion a tool out of it.

Krishnappa made slowly for the sound. Something soft and slippery came under his foot, which sent shivers through his body. From the jolt of disgust and shock at having stepped on a mouse, he jerked his foot back, toppling the bowl. He found the bowl and picked it up. It was an aluminium bowl, dented in many places and jagged at the rim. A rancid stench came from it and he dropped it at once. It fell on the dusty floor.

He was determined to remain strong and not lose his mind as he had once before. So he began to devise, once again, ways of escape. He tested several plans for their feasibility.

The door creaked. He turned towards it. No light came through the half-opened door – that meant it was dark outside, and the night air might be less hot. Krishnappa waited for a whiff of it to come through the door.

Outside, the man said something in Urdu which Krishnappa didn't understand. But he could understand the expletive 'suar'. It was not the fat-faced officer, but some constable who had a screechy voice. He came inside with a lighted match in hand and looked for something, cursing steadily. He fetched the bowl, thrust it in Krishnappa's face and swore at him. He must have been asking him to pick it up. He was a scrawny-looking constable. The lighted match showed his small, dreary face with its big moustache.

Closing the door, he left. He came back after a while, opened the door and said, 'Hey!'

Krishnappa went to the door. The man had the bowl in his hand. The same bowl. 'I don't want to eat,' Krishnappa said in English. The constable put the bowl on the floor. He said something in Urdu and closed the door.

It wasn't even possible to throw the bowl out. Krishnappa felt like vomiting over the stinking sambar and rice that had been poured into it. For a while, he stood there holding his mouth and nose, not knowing what to do. He was sure that mice would come for the food. He picked up the fetid bowl and put it in the corner as before, and feeling the walls with his fingers, made his way to the middle of the room.

There were patches on the walls where the plaster had peeled. Perhaps the bedbugs had made these cracks their home. Feeling his way, Krishnappa found the bowls for water and for toilet. He washed his face with the water, and walked up to a cement bench on one side of the room. The bench was probably meant for sleeping on. He wiped it with the rug, washed the surface with the water left over in the bowl, and sat down. He was too afraid of the bedbugs to sleep. In the corner, the mice had attacked the food.

He was amazed when he noticed how comforted he felt by the mere fact that he had a clean place to sit with his feet dangling off the ground. How the body adapts itself! Just as he was dozing off, he heard a noise outside.

The jingle of bangles and the sound of someone walking in boots. A man made a joke in Urdu and laughed. The word 'cinema' could be heard. The man was merry. It sounded like the fat-faced officer. If it is him, I could ask him for my cigarette pack since he knows English, thought Krishnappa, listening. The sound of someone running, trying to escape. The man shouted something. A woman crying. She spoke in Telugu and Krishnappa was able to follow a little. She really had been to the cinema, she was saying, and that man she went with was someone who was going to marry her next month. She didn't know where the other policeman had taken him. 'Please bring him here,' she pleaded through tears. The man said something in Urdu and laughed again. After a moment's silence, the woman screamed. In Telugu: 'Please, don't. Let me go, let me go!'

Krishnappa left the bench, went to the door and banged on it. 'Are you human beings or rakshasas? Let her go,' he shouted in English. The woman's crying stopped and the man's breathing became loud. Krishnappa kicked the door. 'Open the door! Open the door!' His screaming, as it got louder and louder, hurt his ears and exhausted him. He collapsed to the floor. He realized, with some surprise, that one's anger and indignation could have an effect only if they were directed against human beings, but not in a place like this. It was a new experience for him – a kind of experience which perhaps that hermit had not had, nor Annaji who believed in tit-for-tat violence, nor Maheshwarayya who sought liberation through the practice of mysticism. Krishnappa felt as if daybreak would never come. Or if it came, he wouldn't know it. The mice were scraping noisily at the empty bowl. He had lost all sense of time.

The door opened. As his eyes adjusted to the light, two police constables entered, blindfolded him, and dragged him out, shouting in Urdu, 'Get up, move!' Krishnappa allowed himself to be led. He was put in a chair – a steel chair with arms and a webbed seat. He had begun to be a little at ease when the blindfold was removed.

Krishnappa looked in wonder at the men in front of him, as struck by them as a visitor from another world. Three men sat in a row at a table. Smooth-shaven, each wearing a peaked cap and a crisp, ironed uniform. Before them, cups and saucers of a floral design from which they took tea. The table was draped in a blue woollen cloth, and on it was a glass paperweight. The man in the middle looked suave, educated, mainly because of the glasses he wore. The one on the left appeared to be a sportsman. The one on the right had a greying moustache, and there was a small dot of kumkum in the centre of his forehead.

'Shall I order you some tea?' asked the man in the middle, very courteously, in English.

Looking pointedly at the pictures of Nehru and Rajendra Prasad hanging on the wall behind him, Krishnappa said, 'No, thanks. I am being held a prisoner here unjustly. I am fasting in protest.' A hope that these may be human beings had revived his rebellious feelings.

'If it is proven that you are innocent, we won't keep you here a minute. Please tell us where your friend Annaji has hidden the firearms.'

'I don't know anything about that.'

'You look like an innocent man. It's by getting hold of idealists like you that people like Annaji commit their treacherous acts against the country. If you tell us the truth now, we'll let you go. We want you to study further and be successful in life. Now, look at me. I joined this job after I completed my MA in political science. The gentleman on my left is a Kannada person – do you know that Warangal is of historical importance to the Kannada people, and about the Ramappa temple incident? This other gentleman is a famous cricketer here.'

Krishnappa found the man's words soothing. Especially the way he brought in the Ramappa temple – it could have been a secret sign that, like him, he too was a human being. Krishnappa said, 'I loved Annaji. Your people have murdered him. Annaji was someone who wanted to make our society more enlightened …' After he said it, he felt uneasy. Why did I let myself be charmed by this man's civility and tell him my innermost thoughts, he wondered.

'That would be your opinion, Mr Gowda,' said the cricketer.

The man with the kumkum dot yawned as though all this was not important but just a routine matter, and addressing him in Kannada, said in an intimate tone:

'I am from the Gulbarga region. You are from the Shivamogga region, right? These colleagues of mine are very nice people. They'll let you go. Just tell them who Annaji's contacts were, whom did he correspond with, etc.'

He had drawled the last few words. When no answer was forthcoming from Krishnappa, the one in the middle said in his polished English:

'Young man, we speak to you for your own good. Just tell us whom he corresponded with. We know he had women contacts ...'

'No, I don't know anything.'

'You prolong your suffering unnecessarily. No one walked out free from here without opening their mouth. We do not question you from any selfish motive. It's our duty to our country – a duty to ensure the safety of the country. What did Nehru say?'

The man's lecturing in that grand style encouraged Krishnappa. He fixed the man with a stern eye and said, 'Do you know what your policemen did outside my room last night?' Krishnappa was choking as he spoke. The three men winced in embarrassment, so perhaps they did have human feelings after all. Krishnappa was overcome then and continued, sobbing, 'Those monsters were dragging a woman, a helpless woman and ...' Krishnappa hung his head, unable to speak further.

The man in the middle made a sour face and said, 'Don't get too carried away, young man. There are brutes everywhere. To keep the brutes in check, our people have to be brutes too. Now, are you going to speak or not? This is your chance. Don't expect others to be like us. They won't hesitate to use the third degree to open you up. We have a conference to attend now. All right!' He winked at the constable. The constable led Krishnappa out of the room and blindfolded him again.

Krishnappa was brought to the middle of an open compound around which stood a ten- or twelve-foot-high wall. His blindfold was removed. Here again was the fat-faced man. Krishnappa thought he had been waiting for him.

'Why were you banging on the door last night?'

Krishnappa was silent.

'I know how to make you talk. Do you know what an aeroplane looks like? Tie this man up!' he shouted, and lighting a cigarette, retreated into the building.

In the veranda, two poles propped up an iron pulley. With one end of the rope which passed through the pulley, they tied Krishnappa's hands behind his back. Holding the other end was the screechy-voiced constable, who shouted, 'Sir!'

The fat-faced officer came out, smoking. He signed the ledger held open by another subordinate. 'Yes, proceed,' he said. The screechy-voiced man yanked the rope. As the rope pulled Krishnappa's wrists high up, the fat-faced officer signalled him to stop.

'You see, already it's so painful. If the rope is pulled any more, your eyes will begin to see flashes of lightning,' he said and laughed. 'Speak and be done with it. Poor chap, you haven't even had any food!'

Krishnappa didn't speak.

Suddenly, the officer appeared very angry. 'Pull!' he ordered in Urdu.

When they wrenched his arms further up, Krishnappa felt that they would break. There was darkness in front of his eyes. He had a sinking feeling.

The rope slackened, he felt relieved. He kept his eyes closed in dreadful fear of being pulled again. The pain experienced in anticipation, Krishnappa realized, is more unbearable than the pain experienced while the torture is being inflicted. How to focus the mind on the present without thinking of the pain to come? He let his mind wander to his childhood days. He tried to fix his mind on certain moments that had become dear to him ... In the field, under his watch, the cattle are grazing, tinkling their bells. He is resting under a large jackfruit tree – on a coarse rug. A red robin flits out of a bush, and flutters its wings and flies away. The dancing bird is a sign that he will get to eat a sweet dish soon. He takes up his bamboo flute, but feels hungry. He sees, at a distance, his mother wrapped in a coarse rug, with a scythe in her hand, approaching. As soon as he sees her, he complains to her of how hungry he is.

'What kind of hunger is it? Didn't you have the porridge to eat in the morning?' Mother, smiling at him, scolds him in pretend anger.

'What porridge? It had dirt in it!' he grumbles. Who else could he have complained to about his uncle's wife? That woman was always partial to her own children.

Mother, who is on her way to collect leaves for composting, stops to spend as much time as possible with her son, chattering away and mocking his hunger. As Krishnappa grumbles in irritation, she opens the fold in her sari, takes out a slab of jackfruit kadubu wrapped in banana leaf, and offers it to him. The kadubu is basted generously with rich ghee made from water buffalo's milk. Baked the previous day, tastier today. Mother has secretly saved her share and gives it to her son the following day. He is pleased to get the kadubu Mother has saved behind his aunt's back, but he doesn't show it. He puts it aside and says, 'This kadubu is not baked well.' The mother knows he's being fussy. 'Don't be difficult, just eat!' she tells him, and stands there watching the glint in his eyes as he eats.

Krishnappa is still gobbling down the kadubu when he has to make a run for the wretched cow from Joisa's house. This unruly cow, it keeps straying into people's fields.

Joisa was the teacher at the primary school. Until Krishnappa was ten or eleven, when he began herding cattle, he went to Joisa's school. Joisa's wife, Rukminiamma who was childless, was fond of Krishnappa. She would make him stop by and chat on one pretext or another, all the while gazing at him lovingly. She would press on him snacks like chakkuli and kodubale. Krishnappa's mother would confide in her often, chatting while chewing down a piece of betel nut. In the evening, even if nobody else came, Krishnappa would be there in the front yard of the house to listen to Joisa's recitation of the epic *Bharata*. 'Your son has a royal aura about him,' Joisa would tell his mother. He would notice that Krishnappa's eyes were moist during the story of Karna. 'Now do you want to hear the story of Ekalavya?' he would ask Krishnappa.

Rukminiamma observed the customs of ritual purity to the last degree. When giving him kodubale, she would drop it from above into his outstretched palms. Sometimes, if there was a sari of hers out in the sun drying, she would warn him from a distance, 'Hey, Kitti, watch it! There's a sari drying on the fence. Wait, until I remove it don't touch the fence.' Once, Krishnappa defiantly touched the sari and the fence before coming into the house, which Rukminiamma saw. Just as she raised her hand to hit him, she realized that touching him would cause her mailige, ritual impurity, and she scolded him, 'Rascal!' Seeing her raised hand stopped in mid-air, Krishnappa started laughing. Rukminiamma, stopping herself from laughing, said in pretend anger, 'Wait until I tell your mother. She'll take care of you. You better go home with an areca frond tied to your back for padding.' Then she made him pick up the sari and bring it to the well, and poured water drawn from the well on it. She then wrung the water out of the sari and spread it out to dry once more.

'Ayyo!'

Krishnappa shrieked, but with great effort stopped himself from shrieking again. The rope had been pulled further, it was breaking his arms. As he braced for more, the rope suddenly slackened. Everything went dark before his eyes and he collapsed. When he came to, the screechy-voiced constable was pouring water into his mouth which was held open.

Krishnappa is surprised to hear the strains of a film song coming, probably, from a small roadside hotel located outside the compound. '*Awara hoon ... awara hoon.*' The sound of a moving bullock cart, the cracking of the whip. In the world outside, life goes on as usual. One could sit in leisure at a hotel table and order coffee. Smoke a cigarette. The sound of the bullock cart fades away. The music coming from Radio Ceylon has stopped. Instead, an advertisement for Aspro is heard.

The fat-faced officer stood with his feet planted apart, drinking coffee from a glass. A constable, his hand extended, waited in readiness to get the glass from him. The officer held out the empty glass carelessly in his left hand. The constable, who was standing on his right, walked to the other side to get the glass and went in. From where he had collapsed, Krishnappa looked at the officer who loomed over him like the almighty ruling over his life. Has he got a mother? Was he also a young boy once? Krishnappa wondered. The officer, standing with an air of indifference, bent forward a little and farted. He said something in Urdu, and without looking at Krishnappa, left. A constable got Krishnappa to stand up, led him to a room that had two chairs in it, and sat him in one. Placing some uppittu in an aluminium bowl and coffee before him, he waited.

The bowl made Krishnappa's hunger worse. But having declared his vow of fasting before those civilized-looking officers, he couldn't eat now. Pleased that he had triumphed over this desire, he leaned back in the chair and closed his eyes. Just as he was dozing off, the constable stomped his steel-toe boots on the cement floor. Krishnappa woke up, startled. Annoyed that the constable saw him startle, he kept his eyes open with difficulty so that he wouldn't fall asleep again.

He thought of Gowri Deshpande.

Her dark hair, loosely braided and combed over her ear, has fallen on her chest. She is singing while plucking the strings of the tamboori. She sings the refrain '*Kehet Kabir, suno bhai sadhu…*' in an alto voice. Krishnappa is not ashamed of his desire for her now. He goes up to her and gently caresses her. Afterwards, he talks about it with Annaji. Annaji is pleased. He starts talking about his theory for changing the system. Their society relies on violence. Everything in it having become centralized, it has become a police state. So what's the point in hating just the police? We must understand how the system works and change it. Those who can make this change are the peasants and the workers. The fat-faced officer, too, is a mere instrument. But Krishnappa remembers the terrible cries of a woman he had heard that night when the officer was forcing himself on her. His eyes have lost their sleep, they burn with anger.

Out there somewhere, Krishnappa thinks, Maheshwarayya is trying to find a way to get me out of here. He knows what to do.

There will be a revolution in the country. In his mind, Krishnappa has devised a complex machine with which to punish the fat-faced officer. The machine has hundreds of interlocking wheels. The officer is caught in it, is squeezed in assorted ways. He is being tortured, but not allowed to die. As though in an oil press. Krishnappa remembers the sugarcane press in his village. During harvesting season, sugarcanes being pressed and the juice gushing out, the cauldron licked by the coloured flames of burning areca husks. Foamy molasses being ladled out from the cauldron...

Again, a noise. The constable had eaten the uppittu and dropped the empty bowl. He grinned at Krishnappa like an idiot, showing blackened, bad teeth. For the benefit of his superiors, he arranged it to look as if Krishnappa had eaten the uppittu.

It occurred to Krishnappa that he may be returning to the ordeal of the aeroplane treatment. There is a limit to how much one can endure. Beyond a point, the pain at every additional inch is intolerable. Krishnappa felt his fear. He became afraid that he might betray the names of Annaji's benefactors.

He heard the sound of boots.

The grey-moustached man with the kumkum dot on his forehead entered and lowered himself into a chair. He removed his peaked cap and wiped the sweat off his face with it. The dot of kumkum dissolved and streaked his nose. He wiped his cheeks, neck and nose, careful not to rub the kumkum off.

'You see, this damned place Warangal is surrounded by rocky hills, and that's why it gets awfully hot here. Shall I order some coffee for you?' he said.

Krishnappa shook his head.

'Sharbat?'

'No.'

'You see, this is not something I should involve myself with. It's the job of the officers of lower cadre. In such matters, their approach tends to be rather brutal...'

The man noticed that Krishnappa was not paying attention to what he said.

'My name is Gajanan Joshi,' he said. Krishnappa's lips were sealed, so he said, 'He is your well-wisher, it seems, Mr Maheshwarayya. Came to my house this morning. Had breakfast, too, in my house. And so, I've come to see you myself.'

A sigh escaped Krishnappa on hearing Maheshwarayya's name. He was eager to hear more.

'It's like that in our department. But I am different. I can hardly wait to retire. You see, even today I don't leave home without doing my puja,' said Joshi, wiping his face again. He made a sign to the constable to leave the room, and continued:

'Dealing constantly with criminals, perhaps we too become like them in temperament. Most of us don't even know how to deal with idealistic young men like you. Isn't there a lot of injustice in the country, you ask. Yes, of course. Is it your fault to want revolution? Isn't there a saying: If a man under twenty-five is not a communist, he must be heartless, and if he remains a communist even after twenty-five, he is an idiot?' As he said it, Joshi laughed loudly, and expecting Krishnappa would join him, kept slapping his thighs. Krishnappa sat impassive, staring at him.

'You must have heard the saying before, right? Very funny, very funny,' Joshi stopped laughing, and wiping the tears from his eyes, said, 'Gowda – that's your surname, isn't it? In the Dharwad region, there are Gowdas among brahmins as well. It seems you people were also Jains or Namadharis at one time – that's what Maheshwarayya told me. Very interesting, very interesting. You see, this area was under the rule of the nizams, and so the police around here are quite brutal. That's why I'm here for you. I told Maheshwarayya not to worry. That man, Annaji, they say, had one or two female contacts in Maharashtra. All we need are their addresses.'

Joshi stopped talking. Switching to Telugu, he ordered a constable to bring water. He poured cold water from the jug and offered it to Krishnappa, saying, 'It's just water. What's the harm if you drink it?' and drank some.

'You see, I'm the chief in-charge of this investigation. I have told Maheshwarayya that that's all we need to know from you. Then we will let you go. An interesting man, that Maheshwarayya. You are lucky to know him. I don't know how you, poor man, got mixed up with that character you call Annaji! I tell my son – whatever you do, don't get yourself involved with the police.'

Krishnappa said in a soft voice, as though it was his final statement:

'I don't know anything.'

Joshi got up to leave. Putting his cap on, he said, 'All right, when you feel like talking, send for me. But remember, no one leaves this place without spilling their secrets. It is a fact, I'm not saying it to scare you.'

He straightened his shirt and left. The constable took Krishnappa to the veranda with the aeroplane contraption. There, the fat-faced officer was supervising the aeroplane treatment of a man in rags, who started howling as the degree of his torment grew. The officer got him off the torture machine, noted down what the man was babbling in Telugu, and sent him away with a constable. The constable who had made Krishnappa stop so that he watched this scene, led him through paths that twisted and turned, climbing up and down stairs, through many rooms, and finally into a hall where men in civilian clothes sat at desks, writing. The place looked like any ordinary office. A man who was wearing a white topi below which sacred ash striped his forehead, sat at a desk in the middle, writing something. An ink-stained tablecloth, a bowl containing rancid-smelling glue made by boiling flour, the applicator sticking out of the bowl, photos of Nehru and Bose on the walls, attendants who stood in a corner smoking bidis, smudges on the walls where bidis had been stubbed out, uncovered vessels of drinking water resting on heaped sand in the corners, open cupboards stacked with yellowed files, the din of people's murmurs – taking all this in, Krishnappa made his way slowly through the long hallway, squeezing between rows of desks. This must be the district's main police station, he thought. Joshi must be here somewhere. In the many rooms, there must be his bosses and their bosses. Those rooms must have fans. It was in this building, in one of these rooms, that the three officers had conducted their interrogation of him. These hapless men, turning their clean-shaven faces this way and that way, spectacles on the bridges of their noses, busy with the papers in front of them, they appear to be decent folk. The courtyard where they torture, that must be a part, somewhere, of this building. Likely that the screaming that goes on there does not make it to the ears of these clerks, who appear to be decent folk. These clerks who must be turning the material obtained from the torture into narratives – for presenting before the courts.

The courtyard must be somewhere near here, but where is my dark room? The first step towards attempting to escape – I must prepare a map of this building, Krishnappa began to think. If you have a map, escape becomes easy. That must be the reason why they blindfolded him when they took him around the first time. The room where he saw Joshi, later the courtyard with the contraption, from there going up and down the stairs into several rooms, and then this long hallway where he was brought – they were a jumble in his mind. He said to himself that, next time, he must make it a point to remember everything clearly. When he came out of the hallway, he saw that a bit of the sky and hills of black rock leaning into the sky were visible. It was due to those rocks that the heat in this place was unbearable. Quite likely, the stone for the ancient temple of Ramappa came from these rocks.

When the front of the building came into view, Krishnappa was surprised. This huge building – with its insipid halls, a courtyard for torture, haggard, sunken-eyed, skinny clerks who look weighed down by life's struggles, and a fat-faced monster of a police officer – had, actually, a front that was beautiful! Even in this heat, the lawns were moist and green. There was a fountain where water spilled out of a pot held in the unnaturally arched waist of a female figure. Across from the building, bicycle rickshaws stood in a row, waiting for customers. Carefree peasants chewing betel nut, local people in dhotis walked in the street. Krishnappa made a mental note of the direction in which the building faced and the time of the day. Lesson number one: the pain of the moment is more bearable than the pain anticipated. Lesson number two: in that dark room, he may lose his sense of time and place, and therefore, he must never lose track of where he is at any given time.

Krishnappa's legs had no strength left in them. The pockmarked constable who was escorting him did not seem to be heartless. He gestured to him for water. The constable gave him cool water from an earthen pot that was in the corner near them. On the pretext of drinking water, Krishnappa lingered a little over the front view of the building. The constable rushed him on. The rooms he had passed through were all empty now. Once again, Krishnappa became confused as to where he was. After walking through several hallways, he stood before a door which turned out to be the door to his room. The constable let him in, closed the door and left.

* * *

He was not surprised when bedbugs crawled up and bit him. On the cement bench, rubbing himself, he thought: At least I'm alert thanks to these bedbugs. I am no longer sweating so much, probably because I'm getting used to the hot weather. In a while, his eyelids drooped. He was afraid that they would surprise him in his sleep. Before that happens, I should be done, he said to himself, and focusing his mind on sleeping, he closed his eyes and rested against the wall. Trying to come to terms with the fact that bedbugs do exist, that they do bite, and that it is inevitable that they bite, Krishnappa fell asleep soundly.

When he woke up, he didn't know whether it was day or night, the same day or the next. He was confused. He remembered Rukminiamma: gold studs in either nostril, her braid tied into a small knot with a champak flower tucked in it, she was ordering him to stay at a distance because she was in the ritually pure madi state, and from her spot she was throwing him kodubale to eat. He tried to recall a funny incident that would make him laugh. But it brought up something else that he would rather not think about.

Krishnappa's father died when Krishnappa was still in his mother's womb. As a young boy, he had thought that his father had died an old man, like most others. On the day Maheshwarayya was to take him away to join the school, having stopped his work as a cowherd, his weeping mother sat him down under a banyan tree outside the village to tell him the story of how his father had died.

Ever since the division of their joint properties, his father had had a dispute with a cousin. Puttanna Gowda, the jealous cousin, constantly hassled Krishnappa's father by making trouble, like setting fire to his haystacks. Being a man of strong will, Father would not be cowed by such tactics. Knocking on the door of one court after another, he fought his case and finally won the legal right to the property.

He didn't come home the next day. A boy herder brought the horrible account of what he had seen. When villagers went to look, they saw Father's body had been hacked into pieces and tossed on the ground in a bamboo grove. The police booked a case. Puttanna Gowda was hanged. It was after this that Krishnappa's mother came to live with her brother's family.

Only after he had heard this story did Krishnappa understand why his aunt, whenever she was angry with him, taunted him as 'the ill-omened boy who, even before he was born, finished off his father'.

He had been careful not to let the memory affect him. He had never felt like telling anyone that his father had been murdered, not even Maheshwarayya. But he was not immune to a vague feeling that a dark force had tried to undermine him since the day he was born and that, with determination, he had to go on conquering that force.

How did his father's cousin become so filled with hatred that he wanted to kill him? Do I provoke such hatred in others, Krishnappa thought. When he looked at some people, all that he considered low, mean and dark seemed to be concentrated in them. Thus has the darkness coalesced here, in this place, in this dust, this heat, these bedbugs, this suffocating gloom. Will I be able to defeat it, he wondered, and clenching his teeth, he rose to his feet.

Annaji used to say, 'You can defeat meanness not by the strength of your mind, but by engaging with the world outside, because that's where its origin is.' There may be truth in what he said, Krishnappa thought. But at this moment, I must find a way to transcend the meanness so that it does not wreck my mind. If I must die right here, I should die with my fist clenched. Until the last moment, I should not let my mind be engulfed by this darkness.

Maheshwarayya says, 'Be an Avadhani! Never become tangled in the world. Never lose the ability to bend yourself. Be in the world, not of the world. Eat the fruit, and enjoy looking at it as well. Its body light, its wings strong, its claws sharp, its beak skyward, the bird senses danger even from a distance. It does not crave company, it sings just for its own pleasure.'

He was immersed in thought for a while and felt he had lost sense of time. Next to this room, on the other side of the wall, there must be another room, not a street. Whereas in the courtyard he could hear sounds outside, here he could hear nothing. That fat-faced officer must have forgotten me. Even when I was standing in front of him, in the middle of my punishment, the man would at times lose interest in me and become busy with something else. On remembering this, Krishnappa became concerned. He, Joshi and the other man might have forgotten me, he thought, and might have gone looking for or become busy punishing another victim. Having decided to let me go because I was of no use to them, they might be thinking that I have been released. I wish they would take me out for punishment again.

He rubbed himself, but the relentless bedbugs bit his neck, armpits and thighs. This room was a belly and he was being slowly assimilated.

But these thoughts were a kind of self-indulgence. He felt ashamed. He sat trying to make up elaborate instruments of torture. After a while, he tired of even that. How long has it been since I went on the fast? Three days? Four days? He felt thirsty. Groping his way through the dark, he wetted his mouth with a little of the water that remained in the bowl.

Before he knew what he was doing, in the dust on the floor, he had started drawing with his finger the figure of the chakra according to the creative principles of the Samaya sect. Maheshwarayya was sitting across from him and explaining the steps. Perhaps I am losing my mind as I did once before. I don't believe in god, Krishnappa said to himself, rendering chakras and rubbing away at bedbugs. First, he drew a triangle which would point east. In its centre, a dot, and then another east-facing triangle intersecting with the first one. An opposing west-facing triangle starting at the apex of the first one. Maheshwarayya's eyes shone bright and piercing. The kumkum on his forehead was a broad dot, his hair, long and wet, was thrown over his back. He was in a red-bordered dhoti, rudraksha beads hung across his bare chest.

'The adherents of the Samaya sect conduct their worship within themselves, in the lotus of their heart,' Maheshwarayya told Krishnappa as he prepared the puja. And a chintamani mansion, he described, would have eight concentric walls of precious metals, eleven of precious stones, six of abstractions. In all, twenty-five walls, one higher than the other, each wall impenetrable.

'I am in one such maze,' Krishnappa said to himself, part proudly and part in jest, and burst out laughing. Yes, there is in the centre of the muladhara chakra a triangle in the form of a mandanagara. Therein is the self-manifest, upright lingam. Coiled around it three and a half times, the kundalini is making a sweet but indistinct sound – of the kind that comes from his shaking belly when he laughs. He was now ready to worship Paramashiva Kameshwara and Parvati Kameshwari with equal attention. 'O Bhagavati, without the union with you Paramashiva is immobile.' He invoked the vision of the Samaya goddess. Starting with the coronet and going down, he sang the verses that Maheshwarayya had made him memorize. In praise: the coronet aglitter, her hair fragrant as the parijat flower, the parting of her hair along which flowed the glowing beauty of her visage, as it were; in her lotus-like face, her dark eyes that burned through Manmatha, the god of love, they shone like bees drunk on nectar; her eyebrows that were arched like the arrow of Manmatha; her eyes that could flash the aesthetic essence of the erotic, the wonder, the awe, and the mirth; her nose-ring, her lips; her betel-red tongue, her neck, the three lines of her neck; her four arms, palms, her breasts; her hairline; her navel like the swirl of the Ganga and like the third eye of Shiva when it opens at the end of his penance; her slender waist that seems to be on the verge of breaking under the weight of her breasts; her nimble and wide hips; her feet … Invoking these, he sang the verses in a trance-like state. Gaining his triumph over the bedbugs, the darkness of the room and the dust, he looked around him contemptuously. He tried to bring his mind to the sound of the serpentine kundalini emanating from within himself. This is no delusion, he told himself repeatedly, until it pitched in a monotonous rant, and then he sighed and stood up.

In the shree chakra, where the three lines meet, there are twenty-four secret spots, and twenty-four meeting points where two lines meet. Besides, there are two processes: the creative and the destructive. The destructive process is practised by the Vamacharis of the Kaula sect.

Since mine is the Samaya sect, the fat-faced officer must be of the Kaula sect. He is probably a practitioner of the cult of worshipping the goddess through copulation, fornication, sorcery, through cutting children's tongues, etc. – practices prevalent in this land of the Telugu people. With this thought, Krishnappa burst into laughter again. Soon, he felt his fatigue, and he lay down on the cement bench in the dark and closed his eyes. His dhoti and jubba were soaked. He wished to be rid of his sweaty, dusty clothes. He removed the jubba, and placing it under his head, lay down. He felt like he was floating in the bottomless abyss.

* * *

Time elapsed, he didn't know how much. A constable was pulling him up by the hand. Krishnappa wondered where he was. He went in the direction in which he was being dragged. He recognized the man when the constable cursed him in Urdu in his screechy voice.

It was dark outside as well. But the night breeze was pleasant. Krishnappa walked, taking in the cool air to his heart's content.

The courtyard was brightly lit. In the veranda, the rope from the pulley dangled loose. The fat-faced officer sat in a chair, pouring himself rum from a bottle. At his feet sat two women who had flowers in their hair. They, too, had glasses in their hands. The saris they wore shone in the light. Their lips were red. They had flashy studs in their ears. Their forearms were covered with the stone bangles of the Hyderabad region.

The constable said something in Urdu and laughed. The two women nudged each other and giggled. The officer made Krishnappa take a chair beside him, which surprised him. As he sat relaxed with his legs spread wide, the officer appeared almost human to Krishnappa. Also, because he was not wearing his police officer's cap, his closely cropped hair revealed his flat head. In infancy, a baby's head ought to be placed in a ring of coiled cloth to obtain a beautiful shape. That's why Krishnappa had such a beautifully shaped head, according to his mother.

'Would you like to have a drink?'

Krishnappa's instinct was to glare back. But thinking of him as a Kapalika sorcerer trying to initiate him into the ritual, he softened. The officer might have noticed this.

'If you don't give me those addresses, I will be in trouble, you know? That Joshi will simply write in his confidential report that I am incompetent.'

'I really don't know anything,' said Krishnappa, calculating that the officer, relaxed as he was, would be satisfied with his answer.

'How is it, then, that you've come so far to this place for the sake of that man? Is he your sister's husband, or her lover?' The officer kicked the woman sitting at his feet and laughed. 'I've heard that he was crazy about women. Do you people procure women for your bosses over there, like they do here? Have you pimped for him? See here? They have brought me these two women. First-class whores. Do you know how they part their legs? It will make your arse bounce. You take one of them – and give me those addresses. If not, I might as well forget about my promotion. What do you know about my troubles? I have ten children to feed. I am on duty twenty-four hours, at Joshi's beck and call. He promised the minister that he would wipe out the communists. The minister is a deeply religious person, he goes to the Tirupati temple every week. Having made the promise, this Joshi has put both you and me in a fix. Come now, take this woman.'

He bent down and pulled the woman's sari from her shoulder. When he tried to unbutton her blouse, she stopped him. He stood up, wobbling. Noticing how Krishnappa glowered at him, all of a sudden he said, 'See how arrogant this swine is? Strip him naked!'

As Krishnappa struggled to free himself, two constables held him down and stripped him naked.

'Joshi has told me to get the information out of you today in any way I can. You don't know what I'm capable of doing to you ...' he said and tottered up to Krishnappa. Looking at the women, he prodded Krishnappa's testicles with his stick. 'I'll break your balls, I am warning you!' he said and laughed.

The screechy-voiced constable ran over with more rum for his glass and led him slowly to his chair. The officer burped and barked out an order in English, 'Hey, go piss in his mouth!' The constable did not move so he shouted at him again, this time in Urdu. One of the women came and sat in his lap, and putting her arms around his neck, said something to him.

'Hey there!' the officer shouted for someone. A muscular-looking young man presented himself. Laughing, the officer said something to him. When the young man didn't move, he got himself up, pulled up the other woman who sat crouched on the floor and removed her clothes. The young man took off his clothes. Krishnappa closed his eyes. He got up to run. The officer pounced on him, had his hands and feet tied, and flung him to the ground. With his stick, he pushed up his penis and screamed, 'I am hoisting the flag – everybody, salute!' Everyone laughed gleefully, and now he stroked the naked young man's butt. Krishnappa opened his eyes and closed them again. He heard the officer laugh and prompt the screechy-voiced constable once again to urinate. When he opened his eyes in alarm, the naked young man was hunched over the woman, as the officer bent down to look at them and cheered them on. All the while, the officer had been nudging the screechy-voiced constable with his stick.

Two constables pried Krishnappa's mouth open with a kitchen ladle. The woman started removing the officer's trousers. The screechy-voiced one unbuttoned his khaki shorts and approached Krishnappa, muttering some curse. He squatted on Krishnappa's chest. Two constables held Krishnappa down so that he couldn't move. He held his breath so that he wouldn't swallow the liquid about to fall into his mouth.

Guffawing with delight, cheering the young man on, clasping the other naked woman, the officer shouted at the screechy-voiced constable, 'Are you done?' The constable said, 'Yes, done,' and stood, buttoning up. Krishnappa was surprised and relieved that he hadn't, in fact, done it. After that, the officer forgot him and went on drinking with the naked women by his side. For Krishnappa, things were getting hazy.

When he opened his eyes, it felt as though something soft was unfolding. The chair was where it was before, so were the empty XXX Rum bottles. Though the lights had been turned off, he could see them as if in a dream. The bright stars in the sky were fading. The sound of birds chirping: the sign of something coming to fruition. Krishnappa took a deep breath. He felt an aroma that brought with it a promise of imminent, immense happiness. He saw bunches of marigolds that had grown in the courtyard. He looked with gratitude at each wild plant and waited for the flowers to bloom. The sky was turning red. The sun's rays entered the courtyard. Someone, perhaps the screechy-voiced constable, had covered Krishnappa with a sheet. The light went across the sky, washing the darkness away.

That moment seemed without a beginning or an end. He felt he might have been dead.

* * *

He worried that if he was cast into the dark room, he might lose the time again. But unexpectedly, the door opened. The constable gave him clothes to wear, and then led him out of there. Maheshwarayya was waiting for him in the office. Without saying a word, he took him away in a car to a hotel, where he led him into a room, bathed him, dressed him up in new clothes, and had him drink orange juice.

It was evening when Krishnappa woke up from sleep. Maheshwarayya called room service and had the food brought to them. While he ate some rice mixed with curd, Krishnappa looked out of the glass window, watching the mean streets and the buildings whose colours had faded. Not letting any of his feelings show, Maheshwarayya began the story of Krishnappa's release.

He realized that Joshi was of no use, so Maheshwarayya sought a famous poet who lived there in Warangal. This celebrated Telugu poet had composed an epic on the nuptials of Shiva and Parvati. He came from a prominent priestly family, and was an Ashtavadhani not just in name but in reality. Maheshwarayya was interested in him not only because he was an ardent worshipper in the cult of the Devi and a pleasure-loving man, but the home minister, it was known, was a great admirer of his. The epic was dedicated to the home minister, and the minister had arranged to have it receive some of the highest awards.

Maheshwarayya took a large bottle of whisky to the nightly gathering at the poet's home. The poet was reciting his epic for a group of gathered men, who were nodding their heads appreciatively to its melody. Maheshwarayya presented his whisky and told the poet that he was an admirer from Karnataka. The poet was pleased, and smiling, said:

'It means that my reputation for drinking, too, has spread to Karnataka.'

He and Maheshwarayya talked for a long time about Sarvajna and Vemana. As the night progressed, the Avadhani became more spirited. Maheshwarayya moved to Sanskrit when the inadequacy of his Telugu held him back. The rest of the company were thrilled by their conversing in Sanskrit, not knowing it themselves, and went on swilling their whisky. When the liquor ran low, one of them – Venkataramanayya, a prominent businessman from the vaishya community – fetched another bottle from his car. The night was proving to be a momentous one. Finally, after quite some time, the

Avadhani asked Maheshwarayya why he had come. Maheshwarayya told him about Krishnappa's innocence and his arrest. The Avadhani got up straightaway to call the home minister. Venkataramanayya took them in his car to his home, where there was a telephone on which a 'lightning' call was booked. When it came through, the Avadhani picked up the phone, and at first, the conversation with the minister went on in a relaxed manner. The home minister must have asked him what he was writing at the time. The Avadhani broke out into a melodious recitation of his recent poetry. A delighted Venkataramanayya stood on tiptoe.

Maheshwarayya was afraid that the poet might forget about Krishnappa. He tapped the Avadhani gently on the shoulder as he finished reciting his poetry and whispered: 'The name is Krishnappa.' Perhaps in response to what the minister was asking him, the Avadhani told the home minister casually about the arrest, as if it were an ordinary matter, and he gave the phone number he was calling from, adding that the phone belonged to one of his ardent admirers, Venkataramanayya. This seemed to make Venkataramanayya mighty pleased. The Avadhani put down the receiver and told Maheshwarayya that his work would be done in ten minutes. Venkataramanayya took out some Scotch from a cupboard and poured it for all three. It was past midnight. Krishnappa listened to the narration with fascination and realized that all this had been going on during his dreadful night in the dark room. After ten minutes, the phone rang. It was the minister's PA with information that Joshi wasn't available on the phone, and that the minister would call him again in the morning and Joshi would call back on Venkataramanayya's number. Maheshwarayya spent the night in Venkataramanayya's house. The morning came, but no phone call. After taking his bath, Venkataramanayya left for his shop.

The Avadhani was never up before noon. Maheshwarayya prayed to the Devi and waited.

'At last, the phone call came. You were released. Look here, Krishnappa, they say one should live without ever drawing the attention of the king. But what can you do? It's not possible for someone of your nature. It's what was written for you. Let it be. No point in talking about it. We'll leave this place in the evening,' said Maheshwarayya and sighed.

Part Three

'Nagesha! Nagesha!'

Nagesh, who is sitting outside reading the newspaper, gets up and rushes into the room where Krishnappa is lying prone. Krishnappa is cheered by Nagesh's happiness in being summoned. When they were in the hostel, Kishorekumar used to wait on him like that. He had come to see him some time ago. He was an engineer now, and he wanted help to get a transfer.

Krishnappa has forgotten why he called Nagesh in. Nagesh asks:

'Did you want to read the paper, Gowdre? But there is nothing important in today's paper.'

'What important news can you expect in this country of ours?' says Krishnappa, looking out of the window.

No reaction is expected of him, so Nagesh stands by silently. Krishnappa likes this about Nagesh: he knows when talk is not needed. People like him are rare in the field of politics.

'Did Sita go to the bank?'

'Yes, she did, Gowdre. Veeranna sent the car for her. Gowri went to nursery school.'

'She threw a tantrum in the morning ... ?'

'She didn't want to go to school.'

Tenderness on Krishnappa's face.

'You know, at her age, I didn't like to go to school. Joisa used to promise that he would recite the *Bharata* to get me to come.'

Nagesh pulls a chair up to the bed and sits in it.

'Would you like to dictate? I can take down ...' he says gently, putting no pressure.

'Of course, you will, but not today. I don't feel like it right now, Nagesh. I thought that maybe I could move my leg a little higher, and I tried. I called you to check whether it was wishful thinking or if I was really getting somewhere – that's why I called you just now.'

Krishnappa focuses his effort on his leg.

'Am I taking it higher than I did yesterday, Nagesh?'

'I don't think so, Gowdre,' Nagesh says. He knows Krishnappa doesn't like being lied to. 'How is your hand today?' He gives Krishnappa the rubber ball.

'Oh, the hand!' Krishnappa tries to wrap his fingers around the ball. With clenched teeth, he pushes his energy into his fingers. The fingers fold themselves over the ball's cool, smooth surface. The body tenses itself entirely to squeeze the soft ball. He feels that the ball is yielding to his grip, and that cheers him up. He is happy to see the light in Nagesh's eyes as well. Clutching the ball and savouring the yielding soft resistance, he says, 'I used to be an excellent spinner of tops, you know.'

It was rice-planting season when he returned to the village after his ordeal in Warangal, and working in the paddy field, he would dip his hands into the wet mud to place the seedlings there. Before going back to the village, he went to see Gowri Deshpande once, with Maheshwarayya in tow. She was studying for her exams, and when she came out to greet them her hair was uncombed, her face pale from concentration. She looked vulnerable and beautiful. So recently out of hell, Krishnappa couldn't talk and stood mute, gazing upon her. He hardened his resolve – he wouldn't burden her with an account of his troubles.

'This is Maheshwarayya. I felt like seeing you before leaving for my village.'

Anasuyabayi brought in coffee and served it. She asked why Krishnappa looked so weak. Maheshwarayya spoke delicately of the events so as not to embarrass Krishnappa.

Krishnappa remembers watching Gowri's moist eyes settle on him.

'When your exams are over,' he had said rather formally, 'you must visit our village.' Why hadn't he been more persuasive? She had seemed disappointed by his casualness, hadn't she? Those awkward moments make him uneasy now. He wonders whether he should have allowed himself to be open to the possibilities then, when his life was at a turning point. He asks himself: Why was I unable to speak as I should have? Was it pride that held me from declaring my desire? Was it the principle that I should not hanker for a companion? Or was it that I felt I looked like a skeleton after the hell of Warangal's police station? Yes, he had felt defiled in body as he faced Gowri, immaculate, radiant, with her untended tresses.

Addressing her silence, he asked her, 'What will you do after the exams?'

Perhaps she was disheartened by the tone of this question too. She didn't answer.

'Ye, Nagesha,' Krishnappa says. 'Why is it that we don't have the courage to pursue what we love intensely? Is it because of the fear that once we possess it, it is no longer valuable?'

The question is beyond Nagesh's ken, but he can guess what is behind it. So he says:

'I have written to Gowri Deshpande at her Delhi address, asking her to come.'

Krishnappa's eyes are full of anxiety when he looks at Nagesh. Then a deep sigh. He wishes the stiffness would leave his limbs before she comes. If he gains some strength in his limbs, he will go to his village. He will plant himself in the slushy paddy field again, and push seedlings into it. Under the peepul tree, where he used to graze the cattle, he will wait until flamboyant parrots flock to the guava across.

'It would be great if Maheshwarayya could come.'

'I would have written to him, but we don't have his address, do we?'

'He is like that. He appears suddenly out of nowhere. Besides, the man is now into betting on horses. Isn't the racing season in Bangalore to begin from tomorrow, by the way? He may even come…' Lying on his side, Krishnappa tries to sleep. When will this body become strong enough to turn sides, he starts thinking. By then, I may have another stroke and die. There's a blood clot somewhere in the body. It may clear up, or it may remain there. All that remains for me to do is to live every moment consciously. This body has come to be this way, and it gave no warning.

Who among those that have come into his life has remained whole and who hasn't? Krishnappa can't tell. One cannot possibly say of people what they are by looking at them. Take, for example, Uma. Only Krishnappa knows how devastated she was. She was pregnant when Annaji died. Unable to tell anyone, she went away to her parents' place pretending an illness. Annaji's son must be a grown man now. When Krishnappa saw him, he was cruising on a motorcycle, long hair flowing back like a hippie's. He hears Uma had another two children after him. Krishnappa has kept her secret all this time, hasn't even told Nagesh in the course of the dictation of his memoirs. When they murdered him, Annaji had perhaps been turning away from politics for the settled pleasures of a married life. Was it a conscious choice on his part though, Krishnappa wonders. His death, however, took him beyond such equations. Annaji was the only visionary he had come across in his life. Despite being entangled in trivial matters, his intellect blazed intensely. When he was alive, the question of his integrity used to trouble Krishnappa. Now, he appears to be someone who had died for a cause larger than himself. And Uma? She seems to have gone on living, accepting that which she had to face.

Then, there was that ascetic. Even now Krishnappa doesn't understand him. Was the hermit's inner being burning bright? Or was he, like some vegetables are, hollow inside? Hard to tell. The people haven't left him alone, though. They have built a shrine at his abode. They say that he appears in dreams to answer questions, and from far and wide they come to the shrine, though the hermit never speaks to anyone. Routinely, every morning, he stands at the street corner and recites the Bhagavad Gita. He earns his daily provisions, cooks them, and eats. The routine has continued, but it isn't a simple one any more. Now, the streets he walks are festooned with buntings. At the spot where he stands, they have built a platform and set up a loudspeaker. They call him Siddheshwara. The ascetic doesn't refuse anything, doesn't ask for anything either. But if you see how he has filled out, he mustn't be displeased to answer the public's needs in this way. Renunciation must have got him some pretty nutritious food.

Krishnappa has often wondered why he could never come up with a question that would prompt the ascetic to reply. Was it the state of mind he was in at the time? True, he used to be agitated. Whatever the reason, he thinks with regret, the questions he came up with were perhaps shallow. Yes, the ascetic hermit set a moral bar. But especially when he remembers his reaction in that moment of savagery when the serpent went into the cave, a doubt clouds the picture of spiritual self-possession as he considers his tortoise-like withdrawal from the world. Nothing that he saw in him comes close to Krishnappa's ideal of living, mindfully responding to all the possibilities open to one.

The dichotomy in me, how did it come to be? I must find out before I die. That's all that is left to me, Krishnappa thinks, and prepares to direct his energy to the paralysed side of his body.

'Nagesh, I wish someone could be sent to bring my mother.'

'Do you want me to go, Gowdre?'

'But I need you here. Send one of your friends, will you?'

* * *

A car draws up to the house. Veeranna gets out of it. He's wearing a closed-collar jacket and trousers made of khadi silk. Looks about sixty years old. He owns two big hotels and three movie theatres in Bangalore. Blessed with a natural astuteness, he has grown to become a millionaire, though he was born the son of a small-time contractor. Veeranna is devoted to Lord Venkataramana of Tirupati. He has led the construction of temples for the deity in countries around the world. People are amused by this Veeranna's devotion to Krishnappa, someone like him who is known to be a socialist leader and an enemy of the wealthy class. Veeranna, a man whose favour even big ministers seek, humbles himself before Krishnappa who never asked a favour of anyone. When he had the stroke, Krishnappa lived in an old house near Gandhi Bazar, a rent-controlled dwelling, its latrine located outdoors, paying a rate of a hundred rupees a month. Recognizing the inconvenience to Krishnappa, Veeranna begged him to take one of his flats which he let out in Sadashivanagar. Krishnappa's wife Sitamma joined the plea: this flat was close to the bank where she worked. On his MLA's salary, he couldn't afford to spend more than a hundred rupees a month on rent, and so Krishnappa turned them down.

'In that case, pay me one hundred rupees, that's all.'

'But what is the going rent for it, Veeranna? Seven hundred rupees, right?'

'What do I need so much money for? Besides, I am not giving it for free, am I?' Veeranna implored.

Helpless in his condition, reluctant, Krishnappa moved into the Sadashivanagar flat. In order, also, to staunch Sitamma's daily nagging. Besides, she was happy that the new place was close to Gowri's English-medium nursery school.

It was when Krishnappa had the stroke that people really understood how important he was considered. The governor visited him in the hospital. The chief minister, of whom he was sharply critical, brought in a medical specialist from Bombay. Almost every VIP went to see him in hospital.

Krishnappa was amazed by the solicitude. He hadn't asked for anything. Veeranna too, he felt, was being of service to him with no expectation of a return. After all, of what use could he be to Veeranna? Moreover, he was opposed to the system – nothing against individuals. Wasn't Veeranna just one among many in this system?

Yet, it has often bothered Krishnappa that he has come to accept Veeranna by this kind of rationalization. He suspects Veeranna's humility to be a measure of his shrewdness. His clean-shaven face, the hair in his ears, the bushy eyebrows that join above his nose, his thick neck, the way he tiptoes around him, calls Sita 'Amma, Amma', brings her a fruit-and-vegetable basket from the market – it irritates Krishnappa. In the presence of someone like Nagesh, who is drawn to Krishnappa for his revolutionary personality, these intimacies make Krishnappa feel very embarrassed.

'How are you, Gowdre,' Veeranna says, as he walks in. 'You improve every day, and that is good fortune for our land.' He pulls up a chair and sits down. Krishnappa knows that everyone who comes to see him normally lies about his condition. He ignores such customary niceties.

'I came to see how you are, Gowdre. A specialist is here from Delhi just for the afternoon, and I'm going to bring him over to take a look at you. And yes, since the missus is overworked, from tomorrow a nurse will look after you. Shall I take my leave?'

Veeranna gets up. But just as he goes out, he comes back, remembering something.

'I forgot, Gowdre. You absolutely need a car. The missus has to get to work when she's done with the chores at home. When the Assembly session starts, you'll need to be taken to the House. A taxi every day is expensive. My car is there for your use, of course. But with a car, you should have it when you need it, right? So just sign this form, and we'll have a Fiat purchase sanctioned by the government and it will come through immediately. As an MLA, you are entitled to...'

With a completed application form and a pen at the ready, Veeranna goes to raise the head of the bed to get his signature, when Krishnappa says:

'No, Veeranna. I don't have the money to buy a car.'

'Ayyo! Money, money! Why do you always talk of money?'

'It's impossible. I don't want to borrow the money.'

'That's all right, don't borrow. I will buy your car. My son has been asking for a Fiat for quite some time. If you let me buy the car, I can let you use it when you need it, can't I?'

Nagesh gets up and leaves the room. He has noticed Krishnappa weakening before, in gratitude. To make it easier for him, he steps out now.

Shaking his head, Krishnappa refuses Veeranna's offer.

'All right, you don't want it. But can you do me the favour, at least?'

This man is a millionaire. Another ten or twelve thousand to organize a Fiat for himself since he wants one, it's nothing. He hardly needs to spread his palms before me. And look, he is begging it off me as a favour, Krishnappa thinks to himself as he signs the form without further words. Nagesh comes back into the room after Veeranna has left.

'You see, Nagesh. This, too, is a kind of corruption. Veeranna stands to gain here, at least ten thousand rupees. He says he is buying it for me. Who knows, maybe he is being genuine.'

'Let it go, Gowdre. Is buying the car a big deal for him? He is buying it for your needs. It's an obligation on the part of people like him.'

Krishnappa feels soothed by Nagesh's words. Soothed enough that it becomes possible for him to vent bitterly:

'You are still inexperienced, Nagesh! I am getting soft, am rotting inside. Ten years ago, not even the shadow of such a person would have fallen on me.'

Krishnappa senses that his furious words have elevated him in Nagesh's esteem. He feels disgusted with himself. He closes his eyes and says:

'Will you get me into the wheelchair? There is someone outside, get him to help you.'

* * *

The October weather in Bangalore is cool and pleasant. Krishnappa sits out in the cemented courtyard, warming his bare limbs in the sun and trying to imagine the blood circulating through them.

After Warangal, back in his village he regained his father's paddy field from his uncle and moved with his mother into a little hut he got built. They had two milch cows in the cattle shed. Krishnappa woke up early to milk the cows. Fingers that are lifeless now coaxed the milk down their udders, both hands pulling rhythmically, insistently, but softly. In the beginning, the work would numb his hands. The dappled black-and-white named Kaveri would stand with her hind legs apart, and breathing deeply, relish the flow of the milk as Krishnappa drew on her in a steady rhythm. The milk-stiffened udders would gradually lose their stiffness until they became limp. He would drink the fresh milk warmed up for him by his mother, and make for the paddy field. There, in the summertime, he would drop down to the bottom of the dry well, the water no higher than the ankles. With his hands, he would scoop caked earth into a bucket, which Sheshappa, waiting above, would pull up with a rope. He scraped at the mud until the clogged springs burst open and he felt the thrill of cool water splashing all over him.

'Why do you appease this Kalkutka like stupid people? Throw the stone away. The demon that is harassing you is that agent of the mutth, Narasimha Bhatta. Whatever you make with your labour, he takes away,' Krishnappa would tell neighbouring farmers. It reached Joisa's ear.

On the pretext of asking for banana leaves Joisa might come by, sit at their front door. Conversing casually, drinking the milk Krishnappa had brought him, he would say, 'It seems you told people that Kalkutka is just a stone and they should throw it away. Is that so, Kittappa?'

Joisa's withered body, his stubble so grey, the tuft of hair on his head, and his ever-soft eyes, Krishnappa saw all this and would speak to him gently. His mother would step out to greet Joisa, sit on the stoop and chew her betel nut.

'You had the betel grove as a tenant of the mutth, didn't you? How did you lose your cultivation rights? Who was responsible?'

'Look, we are just the two of us, after all, me and my wife. I get a small pension. Your uncle and a few other Gowda households keep us in firewood, rice, vegetable, banana leaves, fruits – enough to live on – so that they have a brahmin in the village for their astrological forecasts. Now, what need do I have of a betel grove? Tell me.'

'But, Joisre, wasn't it that agent of the mutth, that Bhatta, who reverted the rights to the betel grove and made it his own?'

'The rent was unpaid, and so he got my tenancy cancelled and got in himself. Could it have been avoided?'

'It could, Joisre.'

'I don't know the current law. But I haven't seen anyone who climbed up the steps of a court coming out any better for having done so. Let it be. I don't understand what your inquiry has to do with the question I asked you.'

'It does…'

'Explain to me, then. As they say in Sanskrit: the teacher must welcome being defeated by his pupil.'

'This is how it is, Joisre. Our people trust in Kalkutka. They think that nothing will ever change in this worldly life. They think that it's only through worshipping this goat-and-chicken-eating demon-deity that they ensure their well-being. It is their faith in Kalkutka that has made the gullible folk of our shudra community fearful of Narasimha Bhatta.'

'I agree that your people should rise to the enlightened realization that the divine is without any attributes, shape or form. But that should happen through dharma and karma alone...'

'That's not what I am saying, Joisre. Please hear me out. If people can challenge the writ of Narasimha Bhatta and improve their standard of living, they will gradually be free of goat-and-chicken consuming demon-deities. But their faith in this Kalkutka comes in the way. The question before me is whether to shrink Narasimha Bhatta's fat belly by first daring to throw out the object of worship, that stone, or by first rejecting him and then addressing the problem of Kalkutka worship...'

Krishnappa notices that the brahmin Joisa is upset when he mocks Narasimha Bhatta with the familiar 'he' rather than the respectful one. In the past, Joisa has spoken disapprovingly of Narasimha Bhatta's greed and said in front of Krishnappa sadly: 'If the mutth itself, a religious institution, abandons the path of dharma, what hope is there for the world?' The head of this mutth, the swami, who had kept a woman, had entrusted this Bhatta with its affairs. It disgusted Joisa, who was devout like that. Krishnappa had tried to bring to Joisa the ideas instilled in him by Annaji and the lessons from his ordeals in the Warangal jail. But having failed to convince this brahmin, he had given up. Still, Joisa and his wife had made Krishnappa feel that they were his people. When he returned to the village, the season was cold, and seeing that Joisa was covering himself in just a thin cotton dhoti, he had given him a woollen shawl. It had brought a light as well as tears into Rukminiamma's eyes.

Because he did not eat meat, Krishnappa had further endeared himself to Joisa. Joisa held dear the belief that the rains still came and crops still grew because at least a few brahmins kept up their observance of religious rituals like bathing and praying three times daily – a belief Krishnappa tolerated indulgently. He was aware that Joisa believed his prayers and vigils had carried his student up in the world. Krishnappa tolerated even that. But now his pieties and invocations had brought them to this, and wasn't it a problem that this same boy opposed the brahmin Narasimha Bhatta? For Joisa, however contemptible Narasimha Bhatta might be, he was a brahmin after all, a culmination in this life of the good deeds of previous lives, and wasn't it a problem that Krishnappa set no store by that?

Every year when the time came to collect the yield, Narasimha Bhatta and his men unleashed nightmarish terror on the tenant farmers of the village. That year, there was an incident. A tenant farmer called Beere Gowda was said to owe the mutth, his landlord, a portion of his betel nuts. Into his house went Narasimha Bhatta with his servants, where Beere Gowda's feverish child waited while his wife warmed up some milk in a brass pot for the suffering boy. Bhatta, who had entered the house on the suspicion that Beere Gowda had put away bags of betel nuts, was frustrated and angry when he found the house empty of such a secret stash. Maybe Beere Gowda had moved the betel nuts out of the house, he thought, and gnashing his teeth, Bhatta ordered the servants to throw out the contents of the household. When Beere Gowda's wife fell at his feet to plead with him, he was unrelenting. The milk warming on the hearth was flung into the front yard. The incident shocked the village. Gold studs in his ears, stripes of sacred ash on his forehead, dressed in a gentleman-style dhoti and a coat of serge, the dark, buck-toothed Bhatta, who loomed large with his stick in his hand, appeared to Beere Gowda like the death-bringing god Yama. That night, the child died.

Violence as deeply rooted as what he had seen in the Warangal jail was what Krishnappa saw now, and he led the burial of Beere Gowda's child. He told the farmers who had gathered: 'Bhatta from the mutth has been collecting ever-rising rents from the tenants. Year by year, the length of the bamboo measure he brings gets bigger. You must insist that he use the same bamboo measure as in the past. He will threaten you with punishment. Tell your women to have a broom soaked in water mixed with cattle dung at the ready. If Bhatta enters the house by force, beat him with the broom. It will scare the brahmin.'

The next day, in the home of a poor farmer, the white shirt and the serge coat that Bhatta had on were splattered by a broom soaked in dung-water. The news spread all over the taluk. It led to other events.

With help from the police, Bhatta started evicting farmers. The farmers organized their resistance and went on tilling their fields. They were duly arrested. The news spread to the rest of the country, and socialist leaders from many different parts started arriving in Krishnappa's village to court arrest. Huliyooru became known all over India as Karnataka's Telangana.

Though it did not bring complete victory to the farmers, it humbled their landlord, the institution of the mutth, somewhat. The bamboo measure went back to what it had been five years ago. Farmers became organized. Bowing to people's wishes, Krishnappa stood for election and won. It is now the third time that he has been elected to the Legislative Assembly.

Everyone in the country agrees that Krishnappa has played a significant role in resolving farmers' problems, little by little. Being against them, the government has taken away from brahmins certain landholding privileges that came their way under the inamdari system. In power are the landowning Vokkaligas and Lingayats, and the demand for setting a ceiling on the size of land parcels cannot but be aggressive. Not until now has the government so much as paid lip service to the slogan, 'Land to the tiller!' It's hardly meant that all tillers have become owners of the land over which they toil. Those tillers who have, don't want the others to become landowners.

The struggle for property ownership is necessary for a man's pride in himself, Annaji used to say, and Krishnappa Gowda has experienced it. His doubts are whether the political struggle he is immersed in will gradually liberate man from the humdrum. He is tired of being always surrounded by supplicants, their grievances in his ear. He yearns to be alone. Always involved in conflict, it is with anxiety that he notes he is missing out on the small pleasures life has to offer elsewhere, at every moment. On an evening that he could be alone, he would sit out in the compound of the house in Gandhi Bazar Extension and watch. He would watch young girls in their ankle-length frocks, sauntering in aimless gaiety and would feel his own envy. The complexities they would face in life, the anxieties of their middle-class parents, these didn't seem to bother them. Their braids adorned with jasmines, standing in clusters under lamp posts and trees, those girls tittered and whiled away their coquettish half hour out, and Krishnappa watched them keenly. Some girls turned away shyly if boys looked at them, a few might have even teased the boys.

Didn't some girls in college call me the African prince, Krishnappa recalls. But there I was, always being reserved.

Of Gowri Deshpande in Philadelphia he would think, what would she be doing? Their correspondence had thinned. He'd heard she was interested in politics, her partner was a Marxist sociologist. She argued, it seemed, that parliamentary type politics was not suited for India. She wasn't always like this. Was the stance a borrowed one or was it genuine? – he did not know. He felt sorry that he had never asked her to marry him. Lucina, whom he did ask, hadn't taken him seriously at all. Even those heartaches had lost their intensity. He feared becoming hollow in his personal life. He had married Sita, who could never understand that he had an inner life of his own. Was it when Gopala Reddy died and he realized that he could no longer live alone that he had got married? When his well-wishers persuaded him towards Sita so that someone would look after his needs such as food and other things, he had agreed because he too wanted to marry a woman who was good for just that. It was an uncomfortable thought that something lacking in him turned him away from intense intimacy with women, and that from that fear he had married a woman like Sita. Perhaps Annaji was right to call him feudal. It had been possible to have an intense love affair with Lucina only because he saw no need to marry her. In marrying Sita, he had taken only a domestic maid and not a companion. That's why I lost Gowri, he reflected over a cigarette. The boys and girls in the street outside had left. A neighbour's child was reciting a rote-learned multiplication table. Inside, he could hear Sita grumbling. It was so rare that she had him alone in the house, she was making sure that her pent-up anger reached his ears. Krishnappa went in and sat at his desk with a quarter bottle of whisky, like every evening.

Days would go by, one followed by another. No one remembered the next day what had happened that day. A fiery speech in the Assembly, a fiery speech outside; protesting this, protesting that; visitors seeking this favour or that favour; sign in support of this, against that – Krishnappa wearied of it. He had become friends with a man from a very wealthy family. Though wealthy, Gopala Reddy, who was elected to the Assembly from the Kolar region, was a Marxist. He was lean and trim, and dressed himself in lily-white dhotis and jubbas of fine material in the style of an aristocrat. He moved about in a Benz car. Krishnappa was quite taken with this Marxist's passion for seeking to destroy his own class. When they were once in jail together, he had watched with fascination the man's zestfulness and endurance. Gopala Reddy, who treated wealth and status with disdain, had a cultivated taste in music, cinema and literature. On reading in the paper that Ali Akbar Khan was giving a sarod recital in Calcutta, he took off with Krishnappa in an aeroplane – he was that passionate. He was equally at ease staying at the Taj or in a poor man's shack or in a jail cell. To one such as him, who could enjoy things with an easy detachment, country toddy tapped from a palm tree with a side of chilli bonda fries was as enjoyable as Scotch and cheese. Earlier, Krishnappa had believed that all wealth could bring was some glamour to life. In Gopala Reddy's company, he began to see things differently. He saw that where there was wealth, one's outlook on life and values were different. When he came to Huliyooru to support Krishnappa's election campaign, Gopala Reddy would sleep in the front yard at any farmer's, and in the morning, would eat with relish the porridge and pickled tender mango served to him on a banana leaf. A grass mat, a cap made from an areca frond, a palm-leaf hat, jackfruit kadubu or a bamboo stile – which most people looked past – got his appreciative attention, like the body of a woman he might make love to.

It was only when he went to see Gopala Reddy in his hometown that Krishnappa saw how narrow his world was. He was the master there. His father was a tyrant. The servants could never show their backs to the master. In his palatial house, one never heard the children crying or the women laughing. An absolute silence prevailed in his presence. Gopala Reddy was quite uneasy when he had Krishnappa stay over, even though it was just for that one day. On observing Krishnappa's revulsion for his wealth, Gopala Reddy's regard for him went up. Gopala Reddy knew well, too, that police stations like the one in Warangal existed to protect the interests of the wealthy like him.

Under the broad tutelage of Gopala Reddy, Krishnappa loosened up, became buoyant, and grew. He learned to drink, slept with women. His indignation against the system, which he exuded like sweat from his body, lost its severity and meanness, and developed into a perspective capable of handling things in their totality. As Krishnappa's revolutionary ardour became tempered by Gopala Reddy's sharp intellect, each nourishing the other, women, whisky, musical evenings, travelling in aeroplanes no longer pricked his sense of morality. Being relaxed in trivial matters, not having to scramble for money, speaking open-mindedly, indulging the body in the enjoyment of women, food and whisky – everything was obtainable to Krishnappa, all at once. As a result, he soared high, he felt that he was on top of the highest peak. At times, he would even forget which girl he had been frolicking with the previous day. Only Lucina remained indelible in his mind, the girl with the beauty of a cheetah. Once in a while, he would remember the days and nights of the Warangal jail. But hadn't Gopala Reddy, with his enormous wealth and generosity, mastered the art of defeating life-negating banality? This is how my new life, which I have dreamt of, will be in the future, Krishnappa would think to himself, free of day-to-day worries about money, property, etc.

Once, on seeing the two of them together, Maheshwarayya's breath had seemed to catch. A sari-chaser himself, he wouldn't grudge me my pleasure from women. But what else could it be, Krishnappa wondered. When pressed, Maheshwarayya had said:

'Krishnappa, I'm afraid this is not going to last long. You'll again find yourself sitting under the peepul tree, herding the cattle.'

He was right, his new life didn't last long. Gopala Reddy died of cancer. Afterwards, Krishnappa was in a state of depression for a long time. In the end, he bowed to the pressure from well-wishers and married Sita.

The friendship I got from Gopala Reddy seems like an illusion now, Krishnappa reflects. Gopala was a learned man, more well-read than me. He was a sportsman. He had a sophisticated appreciation of music. He had the skill to make even a woman of pleasure forget that the pleasure was purchased. He must have sought my friendship because he realized that I wasn't the sort who would be awed by his wealth. He must have felt an intense liberation in burning through money, as though it were worthless, in the presence of someone like me. I was his friend, but he looked on me almost worshipfully. To shed my inhibitions, I needed to look at myself through his eyes. Like Maheshwarayya, Annaji and Gowri, he saw something divine in me. He basked in the warmth he had stirred up in me. In his friendship, he made me sing the song of my suffering. As a result, my relish for the bittersweet pain – at times unbearable, which I used to hide within myself – began to wane. The day Gopala Reddy died, I felt orphaned.

'Nagesha.' Nagesh, who went in after leaving Krishnappa outside to warm himself in the sun, comes out.

'I want to go in, it's getting hot here.' Nagesh wheels him to his room.

'Hand me the wallet from the drawer.'

When Nagesh brings him the wallet from his desk, Krishnappa withdraws the two hundred rupees it holds and gives them to him. Not knowing what they are for, Nagesh looks at him quizzically.

'Seems to me you don't have a change of clothes to wear,' says Krishnappa. 'Get some made.'

'No, thank you, Gowdre.'

'Take it. Don't try to be a big shot with me.'

'But that's all the money you have in your wallet.'

'Look, Nagesh, I can still move my right hand. Before it, too, becomes paralysed ...' He sees that what was spoken in jest has made Nagesh sad. He says, 'You are a fool! You don't understand. My wife is a mighty miser. Squirrelling away a little bit at a time from my salary, she has put away ten thousand rupees in the bank. Now shut up and take this money.'

Krishnappa knows Nagesh's background. He is from a poor brahmin family. His father is a petty clerk, always harried. His older brother is an engineer. The sister-in-law is a stingy shrew, and so there is little help from the brother. Six younger sisters, still unmarried. The mother worries that this son Nagesh has given up his studies and is wasting time in useless politics and protests. Nagesh sleeps at the party office, eats here and there. As long as he has enough for coffee and cigarettes, he is content.

Dreaming of a better life in the egalitarian system, which he anticipates will come, he is used to whiling away his time. If you offer to get him a job at HMT, he says no. He gets offended by the offer. He thinks of having a career like everyone else as rather vulgar. He doesn't have any particular talent either. Like many young men, he's influenced by Krishnappa's personality. Krishnappa is painfully aware that his political ideas, his way of living, have dazzled many young men. The thought of these young men growing older makes him anxious.

'Nagesh, I want to tell you a story,' Krishnappa begins, remembering something about Joisa suddenly. Nagesh takes it down in his notebook.

In the period when the farmers of Huliyooru were chasing Bhatta away with brooms soaked in dung, he had to change his sacred thread every day. Seeing as Joisa was troubled by the spectacle, Krishnappa wanted to make light of the attack on brahmins with a joke: 'You should be happy that more janivaras made by you are getting sold.' But he checked himself. It had upset even Krishnappa's mother. So instead, Krishnappa asked in a gentle voice:

'You think of me as your son, don't you, Joisre?'

'What kind of question is this? If I didn't, would I come over to give you advice?'

'He snatched the milk from a dying infant. Was it wrong to thrash a brahmin like him with a broom?'

'Both were wrong. Bhatta will go to hell for the sin he committed. But he was born a brahmin. Why did you have to incur the sin of thrashing him with a broom?'

Krishnappa's mother, who was listening to the conversation, put a wad of tobacco mixed with lime in her mouth and nodded in agreement. Krishnappa felt frustrated with them both. He was saddened that even this poorest-of-the-poor brahmin, a student of the Upanishads and all that, could be so idiotic.

'It makes me sad, Joisre, that you take Bhatta's side just for his caste.'

Hearing Krishnappa so sincerely sad, Joisa was quite perplexed.

'As long as you are caught in this illusory world, such things as caste are your reality, no?'

'Do you, then, feel that I was born a shudra because of my sins? Why do you and Doddamma both feel that I am your son? Tell me.'

Krishnappa had always called Rukminiamma 'Doddamma' – Big Amma.

'Oh, why should I blame you? Scoundrels like Bhatta have squandered the respect our ancestors earned with their good deeds. Legend has it that our Narasimha deity was installed here by Adi Shankara on his way from Kalady to Badrinath. How tarnished in reputation it has become now! The Vaidika Dharma teaches us not to harm even voiceless birds and beasts ...'

Joisa's eyes moistened. One look at the rudraksha prayer beads hung over his bony chest, and Krishnappa's heart melted.

'Seen from a distance, violence done in retaliation looks as ugly as the violence that caused it, Joisre. But you should have seen the glow of self-respect in those people when they felt ready to beat the man with their brooms. Like insects, they had tolerated the indignities done to them, and the institution of the mutth rotted. That's how it was possible for your Bhatta to become the large insect feeding on small insects.'

Dully, Joisa got up to leave. Krishnappa tried to mollify him with humour.

'Even now, our people have respect for brahmins, Joisre. True, they take up the broom to beat them. But in their hearts, they vow to make a gift to Kalkutka in atonement.'

'You are righteous, I know, no? You and Bhatta, where is the comparison between you two? But ...'

Joisa didn't know what more to say, and left. Krishnappa can't forget this incident. He has heard today that the people of his village have pledged a sacrifice to Kalkutka for his speedy recovery. Perhaps that has triggered these memories.

Nagesh says:

'Brahmins ought to be kicked around some more, Gowdre. Only then the caste system can be eradicated.'

Krishnappa starts laughing. Nagesh, in his confusion, wants to know why.

'You're saying that the people of our Gowda community, who grow up eating pigs and goats, should kick the poor rice-and-lentil-eating brahmins like you – just imagining it tickled me. Do you think that the landowners among our caste are quite so upright themselves?'

* * *

'Ye Nagesha! Did you see this latest issue of the *Illustrated Weekly of India*?' Krishnappa is excited. Nagesh is outside, on the veranda, listening to twenty or so MLAs, evening visitors to the house. He comes in.

'What is it, Gowdre?'

'Look.' Krishnappa hands him the *Weekly* with some pages folded back. Noticing the amusement on his face, Nagesh begins to read.

Under a big picture of a hermit, naked except for the loincloth across his crotch, the caption: Sarpasiddheshwarananda. The hermit's long, braided, white beard is matted. In the picture, he is laughing. In another picture, the hermit sits in a tree, scratching himself like a monkey. His toothless mouth is wide open and he looks blissful.

'Remember I used to tell you about the silent hermit? This is him. Read on aloud.'

Krishnappa suspects that the reporter has spiced up the story somewhat. Still, he finds it fascinating. The report has the hermit's rise to fame, a hermit who spoke only to recite the Gita in the streets. As the rumour gained currency that he came to followers in their dreams with words for them, his fame drew people in droves. One day, the hermit disappeared into his cave and didn't emerge. Two or three days went by. Someone from the crowd peeked in to see what the miracle man was up to. A hissing sound, like that from a serpent, came from the cave. The man announced to the crowd outside that the great soul had entered a trance-like state, having assumed the form of the serpent that adorns the locks of Shiva's head. People brought offerings from that day on, to place at the mouth of the cave. The hermit would eat a little of the food and throw out the rest. Devotees would partake of the leftovers, grain by grain. One day, when the hermit did not accept anything, people went up to the cave and peeped in. In the dark, they couldn't see much. But the loud hiss was as though someone was angrily shooing them away. Now the view took hold that the great soul had transformed into a serpent. People started to offer milk.

Three fortnights went by before the miracle man came out again, enveloped in a halo. No longer did he recite the Gita, nor did he speak. Every now and then, he burst into laughter. Or he climbed a tree and sat up there.

Thousands flock from all over the country for a darshan of this Sarpasiddheshwarananda. Stories of miracles abound. Sometimes, Sarpasiddheshwarananda will retreat into the cave to resume his serpent form. The belief is that no one must see him in his serpentine avatar – anyone who sees him thus will surely die. After a few days have passed, the holy man will come out as himself, laugh, and perch atop a tree.

'What do you think of it?' asks Krishnappa out of curiosity.

'Blind faith, that's all.'

'The hermit may be a madman. But don't you sometimes think that he may be a great visionary, Nagesh?'

'It's precisely for such beliefs that our country is what it is.'

'Maybe.'

'What we need is food to eat – not philosophy.'

Finding Krishnappa silent, Nagesh dares to make fun of him:

'Looks like, after falling ill, our Mr Gowdru has started believing in these rogues and imposters!'

'Annaji used to say that to me.' Krishnappa becomes lost in thought. After a while, he resumes in a low voice:

'Look, Nagesh, let's say there is a man who knows for sure that god exists – I'm not talking about a believer in god, but someone who is certain that god does exist. If one can be so certain, then it is not a big deal for such a person to become religious. It's like keeping money in the bank – the interest is guaranteed. On the other hand, for someone to decide to be a believer in god despite being uncertain of god's existence – that is really courageous. In the same way, in politics, it's one thing to engage in the struggle on behalf of the poor, with the belief that the revolution will bring progress and progress will result in the welfare of all. It's the path most revolutionaries take. But after returning from Warangal and before plunging into politics, I could not be certain that only good would come from all the progress we would be making. Even now, I can't be sure. But when I see the banality and misery all around me, the need to fight against it is obvious to me. However, I haven't succeeded in realizing my desire to make our everyday life itself shine brightly. Beere Gowda, who was once being kicked around, is now, thanks to my work, kicking someone else. By this, I don't mean to say that all movements to change society are meaningless, for that would be simplistic. It would be no different to what those stupid people who can't do anything and those hard-hearted people who would like to maintain the status quo both say. But what I'm trying to say, Nagesh...'

Unable to follow, Nagesh looks at Krishnappa and picks up the pencil to make notes. Krishnappa gestures to him to stop.

'It's not easy, Nagesh, to say what one wants to say without letting it become distorted. We are born in this world so that we engage in our karma and strive to drive out the dark forces that undermine life – without, of course, losing our scepticism about the efficacy of our actions.'

He turns his face abruptly. 'Send those people in.'

The party MLAs are waiting to discuss their role in the chaos of defections that looms imminent. The hardliners hold that the rift in the ruling party is not their concern: they ought to stay their course as revolutionaries, without offering anyone an alliance. But there are others, and they are in favour of exploiting the rift to get a new cabinet: they will set as the condition of their support, they argue, that the new cabinet should commit to a time-bound minimum program. A few among them argue in favour of supporting the chief minister. The rest argue in favour of the challenger. One group suspects another group of entering an agreement with the chief minister. That other group suspects that the first group is backing the challenger because he is lavishing them with money. Veeranna, it is thought, is trying to use his influence with Krishnappa to win his support for 'that' group. Most of the hardliners who believe that politics is dirty are those who love to talk – immature, but idealistic. Among the rest are those who have worked hard for the good of the people, those who have become tired of working for the people, and those who are self-serving rogues. Some argue that change is possible only through the explosion of revolution, others that the people can be propelled towards revolution through participation in government.

Although not too keen on a debate, Krishnappa prepares to enter a discussion with those who have come to see him today.

* * *

Krishnappa is pleased that his colleagues in the party, despite their differences, won't go against his advice. Even now, when he is wavering between life and death, the respect he commands hasn't diminished. The doctor from Delhi who examined him said that there was no extensive damage. It was crucial, however, that he undertook physical therapy. As he was feeling cheered up by that, he got a telegram from Gowri Deshpande. It said that she was flying down to see him 'the day after tomorrow'. She had returned from America a little more than six months ago, to Delhi. It has been several years since he has seen her. Now, she will be here in two days. What does she look like now, he wonders. He had hoped that she would come to see him as soon as she returned. When she didn't, he thought that she had grown cold towards him. Pondering whether he felt this way out of self-pity, made worse by his bedridden state, Krishnappa feels disgusted.

Krishnappa is on the bedpan Sita has brought to him, engaged in his morning excretory activities, when who should appear but Maheshwarayya! His breath quickens on hearing Maheshwarayya's voice outside. Nagesh begins telling him about the illness in detail. Maheshwarayya listens silently. He is not the sort to show his emotions. Krishnappa dwells miserably on the shock it will be to the seventy-year-old to see his condition.

Sita proceeds to his sponge bath, soaking a piece of cloth in warm water. Tomorrow, a nurse will do the job. Krishnappa doesn't like Sita attending to him grudgingly, always in a hurry to get to the bank. But today, there is a different reason why her face burns with displeasure. It irritates her when anyone dear to Krishnappa comes to their house. She feels insecure.

'The man must have come chasing the horse's tail,' Sita says, drying Krishnappa's back with a cloth. 'He hasn't shown his face in years.'

In fury, he swings his right hand which is still strong, and has struck her before he knows what he is doing. Suffering from more than that injury, she lets out an anguished, 'Ayyo!' and collapses to the floor in tears. Krishnappa feels utterly disgusted with himself and with her. He wishes he were dead. 'See, this is how he is going to make the revolution – raising his hand on a poor woman!' she whines. After he hit her, he felt exactly the same. As he sits quietly, waiting for her to put clothes on him, he passes the fingers of his right hand through the month-old, salt-and-pepper beard which has grown in the time since the stroke. Only Nagesh, who wants to see him look like Lenin, likes his beard. Letting his mind wander, Krishnappa tries to ignore the snivelling that comes from Sita, but he cannot.

She ties the dhoti around his waist, puts a jubba on him, and plants a comb in his right hand, grumbling all the while. She pushes him in the wheelchair into his room and goes into the kitchen, still grumbling. In the kitchen, Gowri has been crying. Soon, she will be delivered a thumping.

Maheshwarayya comes in and sits down without a word. How he has aged in just a year, Krishnappa thinks as he keeps his eyes on his face. The steadiness in his gait is gone. Bags under the eyes, the skin sagging under the chin. His clothes don't have their usual brightness. There is no kumkum on his forehead.

'Where are you staying?'

'I went to your old house – the one in Gandhi Bazar. I was told that you had moved. On the way, I left my trunk in a hotel, had a bath, and came here,' he says, looking affectionately at Krishnappa.

'People who used to come there, mostly farmers, they don't come to this place. There is no bus service to get here. This is where the well-to-do live – you know, don't you? The few poor people who come to see me are awestruck. They don't sit on the floor and talk on like they would ...'

Moved by his wistfulness, Maheshwarayya says:

'But in your condition, you must have some comfort, no?'

They are both silent for a while. Gowri runs into the room crying. On seeing Maheshwarayya, she stops howling, goes and stands beside her father and sobs. Maheshwarayya takes out a packet of chocolates from his bag. 'Go and give this to your mother. Here, you can have one right away.' He unwraps a chocolate and puts it in her mouth. Maheshwarayya seems to be trying to get at something. Krishnappa recognizes the look as he sits motionless, absently gazing at something, preparing to speak. To give him time, Krishnappa picks up the morning paper and starts reading it. If he so much as moves to exercise his limbs, he fears it will disrupt Maheshwarayya's concentration.

Maheshwarayya used to point to the bird that had made its whole body its eyes and ears. 'We should be like that. The world is right before our eyes, but sadly, we don't see anything at all! To see is to penetrate, to grasp, to absorb at once.' As Krishnappa is reading the newspaper and thinking of those words, a fellow bustles in. 'Namaste, Gowdre!'

Maheshwarayya and Krishnappa look up, startled. Standing before them is Mr Panchalingayya, a coffee planter from Chikmagalur.

'Oh, Gowdre! So sorry! What happened to you? You were hale and hearty!'

Krishnappa feels crushed.

'I know someone here, a specialist. I'll go and fetch him in my car.'

Brushing this aside, Krishnappa says, 'There's no need for that. I have had myself examined. But tell me, what brings you here?'

'There's that medical college in Udupi? The people running the college hold you in such high regard, I was told. I am willing to make a donation of whatever amount they want. Still, a word from you would be needed for my son to get admission. Everybody tells me that you would never agree. That's why your word has value, doesn't it? And by the way, I heard something which made me very happy for you. But look at you! You are lying here like this!'

Krishnappa is puzzled. Panchalingayya laughs and says, pointing to his son who stands behind him:

'This boy, he has passed his exam in the first attempt, though he was not feeling well at the time. If not, he would have gotten first class. He is my only son. What am I going to do with the money I have? Take it with me when I die? He wants to go to foreign. So he is pestering me with his litany of "I want to do medical, I want to do medical". Tell me, what shall I do with all my money? I've decided to either spend it on the good works done by people like you, or for the cause of education … By the way, don't you know? All of Bangalore is agog over it! Everyone in the Golf Club, yesterday, was talking about it. I'm surprised that you don't know it yet. The news going around is that you are going to be the next chief minister! I'm so happy for you! But once you become the CM, it won't be possible for me to talk to you like this, will it? I see you were in the middle of something. I'll come back in the evening. You don't have to say yes or no right away. You don't have to say anything, in fact. I'll talk to Veeranna about it – we'll talk about it in the evening … The doctor, by the way, is excellent. I'll bring him over in the evening …' Panchalingayya laughs and leaves with his son.

'See? This is the sort of person who comes to me now.'

Sensing his distress, Maheshwarayya breaks in:

'These days, I am not able to focus my mind on any single thing. Like a lecher, the wretched mind wanders.' He laughs, pauses, continues:

'I know you want to go back. You are longing to go back to sit under the tree, waiting for the birds who come for the guava. Do you know what I wanted to say earlier? I was thinking – why did my usual intuition fail me when you had the stroke? These days, I am addicted to betting on horses. I want excitement all the time. If I start drinking, I drink all day. Or else I wander around, the way I am doing now. Did you notice how, right now, my mind wandered off? Just now, when I was trying to think of what I was going to say to you, that man with rings on all four fingers turned up ... But it's nothing. I felt that you were going to be all right – and that's what I wanted to tell you.'

Maheshwarayya speaks the last sentence in a soft voice.

'You are not saying this to comfort me, are you?'

With utter seriousness, Maheshwarayya says, 'No.' A moment later, he has cheered up a little. 'You see, it's only at the races that I am not sure of myself. I don't see what is coming. To tell you the truth, my mind has become weak. I will forget this moment in the next one.'

'You come and stay here with me.'

'I don't want to trouble your wife.'

'Please, come.'

'All right,' says Maheshwarayya, preparing to get up.

'It will be the test of my luck today. I'll come back at night,' he says. Then he is gone.

Krishnappa feels quite cheerful. Excitedly, he calls out: 'Nagesha!'

But Nagesh, when he appears, is glum.

'What's wrong?' Krishnappa asks.

'Nothing, Gowdre.'

'No, tell me,' Krishnappa presses him.

'It's my older sister. You know she was working as a clerk? I learned that she lost her job.'

'Don't worry. I'll ask Veeranna to give her a job in his movie theatre.'

'I don't want to use you for such things, Gowdre.'

'Great! There's at least one person who feels that way. Isn't tomorrow night when Gowri Deshpande arrives?'

'Yes.'

'I am worried about where we can put her up. She could stay here, but Sita may create a ruckus. But how can I ask her to stay in a hotel all by herself? Where can she stay?'

'Doesn't Veeranna have a guest house, Gowdre?'

'You see how I am slowly caught in his net?'

'Don't say that. Who could dare trap you?'

'You don't understand – these are the signs that I am sliding.'

The nurse comes in. Veeranna has arranged for a doe-eyed girl. Walking about quietly in her canvas shoes, she massages his left hand and leg in a variety of ways. Gently, she kneads his limbs up and down. She wheels him around in his wheelchair, talking just enough for comfort.

Again and again, Lucina comes to his mind – Lucina who was Krishnappa's companion for a whole year in the days of his friendship with Gopala Reddy. Lucina had trained as a nurse in Delhi. Hers was a tragic story. She came from a middle-class family. A merchant's son from Calcutta had lured her to Delhi on the false promise of marriage. Once in Delhi, he tried to share her among his friends. She endured it for some time, and when things became unbearable, one night she escaped her captor. Not knowing where else to go, she ran until she came to an MP's bungalow and knocked on its door. Gopala Reddy and Krishnappa were staying in that house. Gopala Reddy took the frightened girl in, comforted her, and sent her to a room in the bungalow to sleep that night. Lucina spent the night fearing that one of the two men might come in anytime. The next morning, she went looking for them and found them in the dining hall. She thanked them through tears. Gopala Reddy got her into nursing college. Gradually, she became interested in Krishnappa. Krishnappa had grown fond of her, but kept his distance, being unsure whether gratitude to his friend Gopala Reddy made her like him. She wrote to him later and came to Bangalore on a vacation. Krishnappa was staying in Gopala Reddy's bungalow at the time. One night, she pushed open his door gently, and lay down beside him.

'Why are you doing this?' he asked.

'I like you. You don't understand that?'

'Will you marry me, then?'

'I would like to go to England for further studies. But if you insist, I'll marry you.'

Krishnappa laughed as he held her in his arms.

'But you know that I sleep with other girls, don't you?'

'I know. But the girl who was here yesterday – did you find her so good-looking that you slept with her?' Lucina struck his cheek in playful anger.

'You were sleeping upstairs – I thought you didn't know.' No girl had talked to him so freely before.

'I'm not stupid. Now, so long as I am here with you, I don't want any other girl to come near you. Do you know that ever since I joined the nursing course and started liking you, I have never let anyone come near me?'

'I know.'

As he could see that she, too, got pleasure from him, he was untroubled by guilt. Earlier, he used to get all drunk before he could sleep with a woman. After satisfying his bodily needs in an inebriated state, he would spend the next morning discussing abstract thoughts with Gopala Reddy just to forget the debauchery of the previous night. Lucina made him feel that just being alive was to be happy. In her company, he began to realize how ridiculous he must have looked in his former self, trying to remain dignified even during love-making. Her soft and warm vagina, small but firm breasts, full lips, the oil-brown tone of her skin, the mole on her buttock, her tranquil eyes, her dark hair that cascaded over her back – he would compare them with the top-to-toe description of the Devi's attributes, which he had recited when he was in the Warangal jail. He would amuse Lucina, singing the verses to her. Earlier, having sex had meant a quick ejaculation. Lucina taught him to make every part of the body a fountain of desire, arousal and gratification. Intercourse became the union of the two. It was music that one could make and improvise as much as one wished.

Gradually, Krishnappa became so infatuated that he began to feel he would not be able to live without her. With that, the intensity of his desire, too, ebbed. As he got more and more curious to know why she hated her father so much, he noticed that it irritated her. One day, she told him that her father had lusted after her and her mother had hated her for it, which had made living at home hell for her. Krishnappa started wondering whether her father had forced her. But how to ask? Lucina noticed he was troubled.

'I thought you were different from other men.' There was a note of disappointment in what she said.

'What do you mean by different?'

'Is the present moment not enough for you? Why do you need my past?'

'I want to marry you, that's why.'

'I hate the thought of marriage.'

'Gowri, too, used to talk like this,' Krishnappa said worriedly. But Lucina understood it differently.

'Did she do all these things I do with you?'

Sensing the mischief in her words, Krishnappa kissed her bud-like breasts and said:

'You are just like Gowri. But she could be serious sometimes. You, on the other hand, are frisky.' Krishnappa was trying to hide the disappointment he felt.

'Then do you want a girl who does all these things with you, and discusses politics too?'

'You don't understand what I am saying.'

Where had this Lucina learnt to do all these things? Who was the man who had taught her such things, Krishnappa wondered enviously.

'When you started talking about getting married, all the excitement went out of your body, and out of me as well.'

Lucina got up and went to take a shower. Krishnappa followed her to the shower, and standing in its cool flow, he put soap on her body and was aroused. To fend off his suspicion that he might be taking advantage of her vulnerability, he indulged her with kisses. Wondering whether it was ever possible to have a balanced relationship between a man and a woman, he thought of Annaji's disquisition. Lucina was irked that Krishnappa, after entering her, had his mind on something else. Krishnappa was perplexed, not knowing how to make Lucina understand that there was in him something beyond this love.

In those days, Krishnappa would also feel happy that he had come close to being like Annaji. But just as eagerly as she had made his body sing with joy, Lucina left for England. A year later, she wrote to him that she had married, that the man she had married – Dr Eddie Greenough – was aware of the relationship she had had with Krishnappa and was magnanimous about it. Remembering all that, Krishnappa is amused and feels sorry for his devoted wife Sita that she is so plain and uninteresting. If he had married Lucina, perhaps she too would have turned out this way – who can say?

He looks at the nurse and says, 'Your name? Sorry, I forgot it.'

'Jyothi,' she says with a smile.

'Are you married? Pardon my curiosity.'

Krishnappa learnt the art of making polite conversation with women from Gopala Reddy. He used to ridicule Krishnappa's belief that politeness inhibited the intensity of feeling, and managed to get him over it.

'No, not yet,' says Jyothi. 'My boyfriend has been looking for a job since he took his engineering degree two years ago. We have been waiting to get married for the last five years. He says he doesn't want to get married with no job.'

Krishnappa yields his body to her expert, clinical touch, wondering how a woman can animate this body in so many ways!

'Should I try to get him a job?'

When Jyothi's face brightens up at this as she teaches him to gently fold his fingers, Krishnappa feels great affection for her.

'A friend of mine, Veeranna is his name, is a big contractor. It's he who arranged for you to come to do this. I will ask him to get your boyfriend a job … Shall I?'

Jyothi's eyes become moist.

'Do you know, being jobless, he has lost all his self-confidence? We will manage even if it is just three hundred a month ... Please...'

Krishnappa interrupts her as if to say, 'No need to say anything further.'

* * *

In his mind, he blesses her: 'In his intimacy with you, may his body bloom.' He is surprised to find himself suddenly wishing that, like him, another man, too, should find pleasure in sex. He thought he envied other people's pleasure in sex. But now he feels happy that he is able to wish for this woman standing alluringly near him pleasure with another man.

* * *

In the evening, Maheshwarayya returns, and neglecting to dine, goes straight to bed. Krishnappa gets Nagesh to wheel him to Maheshwarayya's room. He sends Nagesh out and closes the door behind him. He wakes Maheshwarayya, who has been sleeping completely covered under a sheet. It is plain to see that he is drunk, his eyes are red, his face is pale. Krishnappa had noticed in the morning that his hands trembled.

'What's the matter? Why are you like this?' he asks, as though asking the question of himself. He can never bring himself to talk to Maheshwarayya in a pitying tone. He knows how hurt Maheshwarayya would be if he picked it up. Not because he would feel small – unlike him, Maheshwarayya has no need to always appear strong. One of his favourite lines from the *Mankuthimmana Kagga* is: 'Be humble as a blade of grass at the foot of the hill.' One ought to live like the bird – small, without flourish, singing to itself and not to drawing attention to itself. Like the clown of Yakshagana theatre, one should bow and stoop, make people laugh with tomfoolery, and appearing to humour the high and mighty with one's antics, keep one's inner self intact. That is Maheshwarayya's idea of the art of living. When the fat-faced officer in the Warangal jail was peddling excuses to delay the release, Maheshwarayya appeared before him, pulling a long face. Bending low before the officer, quivering, he let himself be seen as an insignificant creature, and pumping him up in this manner secured Krishnappa's release. Krishnappa did not know this until later. He was still in low spirits at the time. Maheshwarayya made him laugh by enacting in the Yakshagana style how he had clowned before the demon king, the fat-faced officer, and won him over with clever tricks. In Maheshwarayya's opinion, the violence done to Krishnappa's self-respect earlier would bloat until it blew up into smithereens like the evil rakshasa bannadavesha of theatre. This perspective helped him to recover from the shock to the tender roots of his life. Gopala Reddy saw Maheshwarayya in those moments and said: 'Look at the clown! How he tends what you call his inner flame! By the way, I have seen this quality in the farmers of my village. They never come before my father. When they do, they pretend they are lowly creatures.' Krishnappa, of course, does not agree with the strategy. Such self-effacement is contrary to his attitude.

Krishnappa thought of Maheshwarayya as insuperable, not someone who would accept defeat. He thought that Maheshwarayya was still in full control of his situation. But sick now, and with bleak prospects of recovery, he is concerned that Maheshwarayya, too, has been depressed.

Maheshwarayya sits up in his bed. He thinks for a while and says: 'No. I shouldn't tell you about myself. It will upset you.'

At once he understands that Maheshwarayya is helpless, but won't seek his help. He feels hurt. Angry.

'You humiliate me.'

Maheshwarayya shakes his head, and looking at him with pity, makes his confession:

It has become impossible to live without the stimulation of gambling. He has tried to calm his urges by sitting at long sessions of prayer with the Devi, but all he can think of is the racing horse. His wealth has melted away. Life has become burdensome. He came to the city to win back what he had lost on a loan of ten thousand from some friends. But once again, he lost everything.

'Is that all? I'll give you the ten thousand.'

On countless occasions, Maheshwarayya had spent on him. He is glad to be able to offer help. All this time, he has not repaid even one paisa.

'I know you will give. But I'll gamble away even that money tomorrow!'

'Gamble if you like. You may even win. Who knows?'

Maheshwarayya's eyes twinkle with confidence.

'Yes, but I may lose it too!'

'Lose it,' Krishnappa says and smiles.

'No. I have a bit of farmland in a village near Dharwad, and a small shack on it. I'll see out my days there, enough of this gambling.'

'If you lose tomorrow, do just that.'

Maheshwarayya, all buoyed up, Krishnappa happy, they look at each other like they used to and laugh. But a moment later, Maheshwarayya becomes worried and utters: 'Bho!'

'This will bring trouble for you,' he says, staring at the door.

'Let it,' says Krishnappa, and calls for Nagesh to wheel him back to his room. He sends for his wife. When she comes in, he asks her to close the door, and speaks. 'Sita, you have that ten thousand rupees in your name in the bank, right? I need that money tomorrow morning.'

She is surprised that her husband, who normally never calls her by her name, has done so.

'What for?' she asks.

'To give Maheshwarayya.'

'Being a socialist, do you think tying money to a horse's tail ...'

'I want to hear none of that! Just give me the money,' Krishnappa thunders.

'No. I have no money to give away.'

Seeing Krishnappa raise his hand, she moves back.

'Yes, you do. Give me the money.'

His mind impels him to get up and seize her by the hand, but his body doesn't move. His eyes brim, his lips tremble. Sita says, softening:

'The City Trust Board has sanctioned a building site for me in Jayamahal Extension. I am saving that money to buy the site ...'

Wiping his tears with his right hand, Krishnappa cries:

'What site?'

'Veeranna made me apply for it, and got it sanctioned,' Sita murmurs, with her head bent. Krishnappa had made a ruckus in the Assembly about those Jayamahal sites. Those sites, valued at forty to fifty thousand in the open market, had been advertised in the papers for seven or eight thousand. When Krishnappa saw this, he suspected that the ministers were planning to distribute the sites among themselves and their relatives. Now, the cabinet of ministers was trying to shut him up by sanctioning a site to his wife. Holding back his anguish, Krishnappa says, 'Sita, you mustn't buy this site.'

'Why? You don't do anything for me. I have a right to buy the site. Don't stop me.'

'Sita, we don't want this site. I'll buy you a different one,' Krishnappa says in a calm voice.

'Sure, you'll buy! If something happens to you tomorrow, do you expect me and your daughter to feed on dirt?'

Krishnappa closes his eyes.

'Go. Go away. I don't want to see you around me,' he says feebly.

After she leaves, he calls out, 'Nagesha!' With his eyes still closed, he says, 'Go to Veeranna right now and get ten thousand rupees as a loan from him. Take an auto. There must be some change in my wallet, take it.'

Nagesh has money for the autorickshaw. He returns in forty-five minutes with a large envelope. Along with the money, Veeranna has sent a note: Here is fifteen thousand. If you need more, send someone for it tomorrow morning. Obediently yours, Veeranna.

'Take me to his room,' Krishnappa says to Nagesh. When he enters the room, Maheshwarayya appears to have been meditating, sitting up in bed.

'There's fifteen thousand here. If you need more, I'll get it for you tomorrow.' Without waiting for an answer, Krishnappa gets Nagesh to wheel him back to his room. Then he lies down in his bed.

* * *

Whenever Krishnappa quarrels with Sita, the child somehow becomes aware of it. Today, she quietly eats what is given to her. Her mother sits her down to straighten out her hair with a comb. Krishnappa watches her sadly as she sits glum-faced, without complaining, even when her mother, in her impatience, yanks at her hair. Her two pigtails neatly plaited and her uniform on, she gets ready to go to school, when Krishnappa calls her to him, 'Gowra!' She hesitates. He calls her again. She comes and stands near him. He pats her on the back. He turns her face towards him and gazes at it. She has his eyes, but has her mother's flat nose. Her lips, which had become swollen when her mother hit her in anger, are now healed. Her nose is not running any more. As she stands there, her face emotionless but showing a maturity beyond her age, Krishnappa feels uneasy. It has been a long time since he has seen her romp around, pulling things out of cupboards and scattering them on the floor, getting scolded by her mother.

Gowri leaves for school. Soon, Veeranna arrives wearing a brightly coloured silk jubba, a stripe of sacred ash on his forehead.

'Do you need some more money?' he asks, as if it is something casual.

Krishnappa says no, and tells him to direct the arrangements for bringing Gowri Deshpande from the airport that night and for her stay in his guest house. He asks him for jobs for Jyothi's boyfriend and Nagesh's older sister. 'Fine,' Veeranna says to everything – none of it is a big deal. Veeranna informs him that Panchalingayya came to see him, and that he told Panchalingayya not to bother Krishnappa Gowda about things like college seats and that he would arrange for a seat for the boy.

'You need to get well soon,' he says.

The words, though not unusual, seem charged, the way he says them. Krishnappa asks:

'It seems you have something else on your mind? Say it.'

'I don't want to discuss it now because you shouldn't be bothered about it. The day you'll have to shoulder a big responsibility is not very far.'

'I have heard this. But you see, I will not enter into an alliance with those who switch their parties.'

'Don't. Form your own cabinet of ministers. You would like to introduce the new Tenancy Act, wouldn't you? Do it. Those who want to support you will do so. If not, you can give your resignation then ... Look at me, telling you what to do! Sorry, forgive me.'

'Veeranna, I want to ask you one thing. Why did you get Sita to apply for a site?'

'Now you are joking! Isn't she a citizen of this country?' Veeranna laughs. But Krishnappa is serious, and on seeing this he says soberly:

'Gowdre, no matter how great a man you are, women understand only things like this. Why blame them? Do you think they want it for themselves? The female has the responsibility of building the nest. Our work is to fly above in the vast sky. Isn't this what dharma is?'

'No matter what your spin, this is also corruption.'

'Shiva! Shiva! What you are saying is quite funny! If your wife buys a site with her hard-earned money, it is corruption? But people like us, who have to conduct business using speed money and such – what would you call that? Each according to his dharma, perhaps?'

'No. I am saying that what you are doing is wrong.'

'If it's wrong, let it be so. How will it be set right? When people like me are set right? Or when the country is set right? Take the PWD. Without it being set right, can I set myself right? Tell me. Who is to set everything right, top to bottom? It's people like you! That's why I'm telling you: you should become the leader, form the cabinet. Now, I must go. I have work to do at the cinema theatre. Shall I take your leave?'

Veeranna leaves. This Veeranna, he praises me to the sky or stands meekly before me with folded hands, and even so has gained total influence over me. He lets me object, be unyielding, be angry, and by praising me for it, plans to win me over ultimately. I can't be sure if the ploy is only for his benefit. He got the contract for an irrigation project through the chief minister, didn't he? Well, if not Veeranna, some other fellow would have secured that contract.

Krishnappa sits in the wheelchair confused, unable to fathom Veeranna's depth and breadth, when Jyothi comes in. Moving quietly, she puts a new sheet on the bed, arranges the roses she has brought with her in the vase, and expertly lays him down on the bed. Cheerfully massaging him, she begins the story of a movie she saw the previous evening. In the way she narrates the story of the lovers' separation, she hints at her own inner self and the yearning there. She seems to think she has done the right thing by remaining a closed bud to her hero until he can find a job, which leaves Krishnappa incredulous. She is cheerful today because her boyfriend is going to get a job. Perhaps she will open herself to him tonight. The thrill of anticipation pulses from her soft hands through his sluggish shoulder, arms, sides, waist, thighs and legs. Krishnappa feels as though he is drawing healthfulness from the very air around him.

His attention snags on a rose that has blossomed larger than the others in the vase. Its petals of deep pink glisten moistly, the petals now revealing, now hiding in the folds of their curls the alluring mystery of its soft, small centre, an immaculate beauty set against jagged leaves and a thorny stem. Contemplating the rose, Krishnappa listens to Jyothi's sweet chatter. The rose is a flame that burns coolly. As it teases – now revealing, now concealing – he can't bear to look at it. He looks at Jyothi's face. Pressing and kneading his body with ease, she seems pleased with her own chatter. He remembers that sometimes he would wish for an easy death. But now, he wishes that his leaden body could be reinvigorated. He wants to climb the trees, go into the well and dig up the water-clogging mud, swim in the river, do the planting in the paddy field, take the flower-soft chicks in his palms – he wants to do many such things. Wasn't I pretending not to hear what Veeranna was saying, Krishnappa thinks. He hopes that political power might bring back the vitality to his lifeless body. He remembers the jackfruit kadubu his mother would bring him, hidden in the folds of her sari.

He sees that Nagesh has come in with a gloomy face.

'What's wrong?' he asks. Jyothi says she will come back in the evening, and gets up to leave. Nagesh doesn't answer. Krishnappa gets annoyed because Nagesh is trying to avoid his gaze. Glumly, Nagesh hands him a ten-paisa tabloid called *Kidi*, which he brings out of his pocket, and says: 'The bastards! Writing all kinds of things! But don't mind them, please!'

Krishnappa reads. Under the heading 'Krishnappa Gowda Plotting to Become Chief Minister', there is a whole litany of allegations – the kind of allegations no one, until now, has made against him: about the site he has gotten in his wife's name, in Jayamahal Extension. Knowing full well that the present government has sanctioned the contract for a reservoir project worth millions of rupees to one Veeranna after modifying the terms of the contract in his favour, why does Krishnappa keep silent? How is it that his only close friends are people like the wealthy landowner the late Gopala Reddy, and this moneybag Veeranna? Is it true that, on getting a Fiat sanctioned for himself, Krishnappa has given the car to Veeranna's profligate son for his nightly activities? Is it only a rumour that Mr Gowda's wife, who is an ordinary clerk in a bank, is being promoted to the position of the manager? Rumour has it that, with the ruling party about to break up, the present chief minister's faction is trying to hold on to power by making Mr Gowda, known to be a revolutionary, their leader and the chief minister. How much money is Mr Veeranna spending behind the scenes to manoeuvre the MLAs? Is it true that Mr Veeranna is also spending a lot of money to buy the left-wing faction of Mr Gowda's group which is opposed to the chief minister? Is it true that, to get the chief minister's position, Mr Gowda, well known as a rationalist intellectual, is resorting to sorcery and magic with the help of one Mr Maheshwarayya who practises the rituals of the Shakta cult? Beating his wife, sleeping with vulnerable young women, drinking, using demagoguery to oppose the corrupt system – are these really the ways of a revolutionary? How has a man born into a family of farmers who at one time really toiled as indentured tenants, become a puppet of the corrupt and the wealthy? The article ends on a note of sadness on the part of its author. The last sentence, printed in bold type, cleverly tries to insinuate how, for both Mr Gowda and his opponents, his illness itself has become the means of exploiting the sentiments of the people.

Watching Krishnappa's face pale as he reads, Nagesh tries to cheer him up.

'This is the work of that Nagaraj, Gowdre.'

'It's true Nagaraj is opposed to me, but he is not the sort who would write anonymous articles in the papers,' Krishnappa says.

'There's no doubt that he has written it. To you, everything that looks white is milk ...'

'Ask him to come and see me. And before you go, get me the writing pad and pen.'

Nagaraj, with his rigid principles and uncompromising nature, reminds Krishnappa of himself in his youth. The difference is that he had entered politics unwillingly, seeing no other way of making life worthwhile, whereas Nagaraj can't see beyond politics. He thinks that, to make life meaningful, there is no other way but to be a revolutionary. Chain-smoking Charminars, he goes about antagonizing everyone with his provocative talk. Colleagues, who listen to Krishnappa patiently even though he says the same things with the same fervour, pounce on Nagaraj whenever he opens his mouth. The son of a wealthy criminal lawyer, he became a Marxist while studying at the Delhi School of Economics. But being opposed to the pro-Soviet Union policy of the Communist Party of India, he saw no choice except to join the socialists, though he didn't care much for the socialist faction either. He openly admits that he has joined them only for the time being. The others tolerate him because he has been elected to the Assembly from the Tumkur farmers' constituency with a thumping majority. They keep bringing rumours to Krishnappa that Nagaraj is competing with him for the leadership. Nagaraj cannot stand Krishnappa behaving as though he is without equal. There are times when, in the party meetings, Nagaraj has jeered at Krishnappa, calling him feudal. Because of his unwillingness to make any compromise with the ruling party, Krishnappa has often told him, 'Your way of thinking is: until we are able to share the sky, what is the point of sharing the earth?' Then Nagaraj will retort bitterly: 'Mao was right, a revisionist is more dangerous than an enemy.' At times, Krishnappa has secretly wished that this Nagaraj will grow soft and make some compromising mistake. But having turned his back on a life of comfort and ease, Nagaraj lives unencumbered, alone, like a ghost. Adhering to his principles, limiting his life's aim to achieving a single purpose, he burns like a red-hot iron rod. Krishnappa will at times become envious of him, and become perplexed, too, by his immaturity. Krishnappa reads what has been written once more. He puts the writing pad over it and waits for Nagaraj. Nagaraj arrives, scruffy in a wrinkled jubba and trousers, his head bent slightly. Glowering, he walks in, pulls up a chair and sits in it. Krishnappa gestures to Nagesh to leave the room and close the door.

Nagaraj doesn't so much as bother to ask after Krishnappa's health. He is truly a caricature of my younger self, Krishnappa thinks. He gives the newspaper to Nagaraj.

'I've seen it,' he says.

'People might say it is you who got this in.'

'As long as you don't believe it, it's okay.'

Nagaraj speaks in a straightforward way. A few days ago, in the party meeting, after remaining silent until the end, he said:

'This is the trouble with parliamentary politics. No matter what faction we join to form a government, nothing can be achieved. The state is always the instrument of the ruling class. It is not possible to use the state in any other way in a parliamentary set-up.' The others reacted angrily to what he said.

'What are you going to do about it, then?' they challenged him.

'Who, me? When our party forms the government, I will stay out of it. Perhaps I'll resign my membership in the Assembly as well. I don't have a clear position yet.'

'If that's your view of parliamentary politics,' Krishnappa told him provocatively, 'it is not ethically right for you to keep waiting to see how the wind blows. If you do, you are deceiving yourself.'

'There is truth in what you say. I haven't yet become totally free from the delusions of my class.' The straightforwardness with which Nagaraj spoke made people laugh. But it touched Krishnappa. He has thought of it often.

Remembering it now, Krishnappa says calmly:

'After reading this article, I felt I should ask you: do you also feel about me this way? I am asking because I myself am confused.'

'The question of individuals is not important here. In this system we are in, to say who is honest and how honest he is, is all relative. I, too, worry that the system will snare you in its web. You have a certain image, and the system relies on that image to save itself.'

'What do you think I should do, then? Although I don't agree with your ideology, I do want your advice in this matter.'

'If our party had followed the straight path until now, people like Veeranna would not have sought you out – don't you think?'

Krishnappa gets angry at once:

'Nagaraj! True, Veeranna has helped me. But I never put out my hand for help. You were born in a wealthy family. If you had been born and had grown up poor like me, I wonder whether you would have remained as honest as I have.'

Nagaraj doesn't get angry:

'You are talking like an individualist. You don't have ideological clarity. Anyway, that was not my question at all. Tell me, if I had been true to myself, would I be where I am?'

'The prime minister of the country is trying to become a dictator. If the prime minister's party comes to power here in our state, what little civil rights we have will vanish. It is true that the present chief minister is a reactionary. But don't you think that, with his support, if we form a government committed to a time-bound programme, we may be able to accomplish something?'

'No. Only when the situation in the country gets still worse will people lose their faith in the parliamentary system. I don't like the idea of doing patchwork in the meanwhile.'

Krishnappa is quiet for a moment and then says:

'I don't agree with you. Your idea of setting fire to the existing house to warm yourself is half-baked and immature. However, my problems are of a personal nature – having to do with my integrity. I sent for you to talk about it. If you, too, think that I have let myself be caught in someone's net, here is the letter of my resignation from my membership of the Assembly. Take it with you, think coolly for an hour, and if you think it is the right thing to do, post it to the speaker.'

He gives the letter to Nagaraj. Nagaraj stands up, and showing no emotion, says:

'Being an individualist, you worry too much about your integrity. It is a kind of sickly self-indulgence. If it's a question of integrity ... you are a greater man than me ... closer to the people than I am. That's why your being who you are is important to me. So your resigning on the issue of whether you have remained pure or not is, in my view, irrelevant. How is it possible to remain pure in a bourgeois society? What you now need clarity about is whether or not the parliamentary way is the right one.'

Giving back Krishnappa's letter, he continues in a dry tone:

'That's why your experience is important. I am still a raw person. Do you really think that to stop fascism, it is necessary, for the time being, to have the parliamentary way? When you come to a decision in this matter, let me know. Because even my intolerance may be an adventurist indulgence. Therefore, we need your direction, as you are someone who is in touch with the people.'

Nagaraj seems confused about what he is saying. He stands quietly for a moment then makes off without even taking leave.

His words affect Krishnappa greatly.

As I am on the threshold between life and death, I must now decide: Is my becoming the chief minister of the state necessary to break the fascist conspiracy? Is this the desire of a dying man to regain his vitality through political power? Or is it the wish to put an end to the kind of cruel display of power which I saw in the Warangal jail? Can the class interests of people like Veeranna stand up to fascism? By asking all these questions, am I intellectually justifying my own self-interest?

'You are a fool, Nagaraj! A great fool! You don't understand life's complexity. I may want to overlook Veeranna's class interests so that tonight Jyothi and her boyfriend can experience the secret pleasures of their bodies,' Krishnappa feels like screaming. 'What else is there in life, you fool, except to eat, sleep, weld the bodies in love-making, and when the little fellow between your legs goes limp, get your kick by chasing the horse's tail?'

Krishnappa holds his breath and tries to move the leg that Jyothi has massaged.

* * *

It is now five thirty. Gowri's flight is at six. Nagesh should be able to recognize her from a photo he has seen of her in a white sari. Betraying no excitement, she will inquire in her refined manner, 'How is Gowdru?' Nagesh will bring her here in Veeranna's car, and later take her to the guest house. On the way, he will tell her about me: that I had a stroke, that I am likely to become the chief minister, that though I don't desire it, I may even accept it on principle. It will take at least a half hour from the airport. What if the flight is delayed? Or if she wants to first go to the guest house to change?

A car pulls in. Did the plane arrive early? Footsteps. But not a woman's footsteps.

'Namaste.'

Standing before him, with Veeranna, are Narasimha Bhatta and Rame Gowda: Narasimha Bhatta, who had thrown out the milk being warmed up for a child, and with him Rame Gowda, who had stood against Krishnappa in the election as the landowners' candidate.

The three sit down and chatter on: 'You are the great leader. May god give you health, for the good of the land,' and so on.

'What little understanding I had of the Tenancy Act then,' Narasimha Bhatta goes on. 'We can't afford to practise the policy of "might is right" any longer, can we? Thanks to Krishnappa Gowda's hard-fought campaign, it's now possible for me to own a betel-nut grove that belonged to the mutth before. The swami and I are not on good terms. How can my sons be expected to spend their lives doing priestly jobs like I did, performing pujas and other chores? I have to get them educated, don't I?' For his children's education, Bhatta has set up a house in the town of Shivamogga. To make matters worse, he has diabetes. Needs a daily injection. After setting up his own brother-in-law as the manager of the affairs of the mutth, he has moved to the town. How unjust of the swami to ask him to give back the land – a paltry ten acres of areca grove which, in recognition of his having served the swami, had been leased to him for cultivation? At least the swami could have appointed Bhatta's son – a boy who had the looks and features for it – as his successor. Instead, he appointed an older sister's son. But for the Tenancy Act which got passed thanks to Krishnappa Gowda's efforts, the grove that Narasimha Bhatta got in the end would not have become his. Same with Rame Gowda – he got to be the owner of the areca grove because of this Act. Some people had whispered ideas in their ears against Krishnappa Gowda: 'If he wins, he will make you go around with a begging bowl in hand.' Now, everyone knows what the truth was.

'What brings you here?'

Krishnappa is feeling tired. Veeranna explains: The farmers of Krishnappa's constituency have arranged a week-long felicitation ceremony for him. Every night, there is to be a Yakshagana performance. During the day, there will be speeches – on issues concerning the farmers. On the opening day, Krishnappa will be presented with a fund of one lakh rupees, a fund to which the farmers have contributed one or two rupees each. Krishnappa Gowda's popularity is such that even Chandrayya – the chief minister's archenemy – has shown interest in attending the event. On the whole, it is going to be a festive occasion for the poor farmers of the land. The leaders of Krishnappa Gowda's party in Delhi are also expected. To keep this a surprise for Gowdru, all this time his supporters have been making behind-the-scenes preparations.

To Veeranna's velvety speech, Narasimha Bhatta with the diamond ear-studs and Rame Gowda with the new dentures add their profusion of sentiment. Interrupting them, Krishnappa says, 'Veeranna, will you find out whether Gowri Deshpande's flight has arrived?'

Veeranna gets up to leave, but hearing the sound of a car outside just then, he sits down and says, 'It must be her. Please have her taken to the guest house.'

'I must talk to her now. I'll send her afterwards,' Krishnappa says and waves goodbye with his right hand. Bhatta, Rame Gowda and Veeranna bow to take their leave.

* * *

Krishnappa can scarcely believe his eyes. Gowri stands before him in blue jeans and a fine Lucknow-style kurta. She has tied her long hair with a kerchief and let it fall on her back. Except for a few grey lines that streak her hair here and there, she is the same Gowri. The same slim build, the same shining eyes. Curbing her excitement, she says with a laugh:

'You don't look like an African prince now. In your beard, you look like an African god. You have become a shade lighter too, probably because of staying indoors all the time.'

Krishnappa sits in his wheelchair, unable to speak. His eyes tear up. He is unconcerned that Gowri should notice his emotion, which may suggest he has lost his youthful pride and stiffness. He could have said to her, when she was getting ready to go to America, 'I want you, please don't go.' But he didn't. In those days, he used to be too restless to know clearly what he wanted. Now all he can do is lift his right hand – which he does. Gowri stands to his right and presses his head to her belly, passing her fingers through his curly hair. Her belly becomes wet with his tears. Krishnappa holds her tight with his right hand.

'Why didn't you come soon after you arrived in Delhi?' he asks.

'I didn't know whether you wanted me to or not,' she says with seriousness, but to temper it, adds light-heartedly, 'I was waiting for your pride to cool down.'

Both laugh. Gowri sits down and looks around the room. Noticing her eyes linger on the roses, he remembers the rose garden in her front yard. Gowri, too, thinks of the day when Krishnappa sat watching the roses in her garden from her drawing room. As though she has read his mind, she says:

'Nanjappa died, you know? My mother lives with me in Delhi.'

'Do you like your work?'

'Yes. My book on Rimbaud is being published.'

Her voice has the same mix of shyness and seriousness as before. Seeing Krishnappa's eyes devouring her face, she turns red like a young girl. To distract him, she says:

'In America, I married a sociologist. Well, rather, I lived in with him. A nice man – a Marxist – he took part in Martin Luther King's civil rights movement. So did I. Do you know that I, too, am now interested in politics? I belong to a group in Delhi. We fear that our prime minister is becoming a dictator. You must, somehow, see to it that the people from the prime minister's party don't come to power here. Nagesh told me everything. The situation is getting to be exciting ... Look at me, I was telling you about Eddy but got sidetracked. May I smoke?'

Still the same Gowri, Krishnappa thinks – to hide her deeper feelings, she starts talking about all sorts of things. Sometimes, just to be provocative, she is contrary. Gowri takes a cigarette from her packet and lights it.

'Do you still smoke?' she asks.

'I have given it up,' he says. 'But if you give me one, I'll smoke.' Krishnappa could never have imagined that Gowri would be smoking someday.

'If you don't mind,' she says, and puts the cigarette from her mouth to his lips. As he is trying to get used to her, she says, 'Have you remained a feudal still? I hope not. Are you shocked to see that I smoke?' Tilting her head back, she lifts her hair with her hand, lets it fall over her back, and laughs. Even this gesture is new. Do I find it unnatural? Or is it my way of looking, Krishnappa wonders. Gowri gives him a mischievous look, then becoming sober, says:

'Pretty soon, I became disillusioned with the American male. I called you feudal. But when it comes to women, they too are feudalistic. Despite being a Marxist, unconsciously, Eddy continued to be feudal. But we remain friends still.'

Krishnappa is downcast. She wants to ask him if he is hurt. She is pleased to note that her American affair has hurt him. After a beat, without letting on, she says:

'Where are your wife and daughter?'

For a minute, Krishnappa doesn't answer. When he speaks, he says slowly, his head bent:

'I may die any day now, Gowri. Why should I pretend in front of you? I have a wife in name only. I beat her.'

She may understand my pain, he thinks. She is quiet.

'Nagesha!' Krishnappa calls out. Nagesh is all eagerness as he comes in.

'They are going to bring out a biography of yours at the felicitation ceremony. I've started writing it. When you were made the president of the Bihar Kisan Conference, then ...'

Krishnappa laughs, and interrupting him, says, 'Write, by all means, write. But right now, ask Sita to come here. Bring Gowri also.' Seeing her surprise, he says, 'I named my daughter after you.'

After some time, Nagesh brings Gowri and says:

'Sitamma has a headache it seems. She is lying down. Gowdre, having been born in remote Malnadu, you became the leader of the peasants for the whole of India – we need to highlight it in your biography. That's what I feel.' Krishnappa feels embarrassed by Nagesh's exuberance. Gowri, who notices it too, holds the child's hand and caresses her face.

'She has your eyes,' she says.

Krishnappa sees that the child has again been traumatized into silence by her mother. Usually, she won't let anyone near her. But here she is being hugged by a stranger, and one in trousers at that.

'Sweet child!' Gowri says, lighting another cigarette. He sees she is perturbed but is not showing it. He says, 'You should go to the guest house now and come back tomorrow. You need to rest.' He suspects that inside the house, his wife is probably sobbing. Can her sobbing, which only reaches my ears, be heard by Gowri? Can Nagesh hear it? But when he sees Nagesh's face beaming from imagining him being taken in a procession by the farmers of Bihar, Krishnappa feels the absurdity of it.

'You should rest, too. Bye!' says Gowri, and leaves with Nagesh. Krishnappa quietly pats the child. Unawares, he is doing his movement exercises for the left side. Yes, he can hear his wife's sobs. Once again, the wish to die sprouts within him.

* * *

The next morning, Jyothi walks in cheerfully, holding a bouquet of flaming red roses, dressed in a white sari and blouse. Her boyfriend has started his job. Before Krishnappa can utter a word, she says, 'He's waiting in the autorickshaw. He wants to come in to thank you.' On gaining Krishnappa's consent, she runs out and brings her boyfriend back with her, an athletic young man with a handsome moustache.

'This is Edwin,' she says.

'Congratulations,' Krishnappa says with a mix of envy and happiness, extending his right hand. Edwin shakes it forcefully, expresses his gratitude, and is soon off. Krishnappa, looking at Jyothi, who is absorbed in arranging the roses in a vase, notices a blissful languor in her walk and says with a smile, 'Did you celebrate the job yesterday?'

Indicating 'yes' just by a gesture, she continues to arrange the flowers and blushes at Krishnappa's quiet smile. She turns around, and in pretend anger, tiptoes across to him.

'Don't be naughty!' she says and pinches his cheek. In the next moment, wide-eyed in mock fear for what she had done, she bites her lip.

'Are you ready for the pan?' she asks in her unemotional, professional tone. When her experienced hands reach out to cleanse and wash him, he marvels at her expert handling, and like a child, he yields to her nimble, firm touch. She handles his bodily functions – disgusting as they are to him – as if they were ordinary. After giving him a sponge bath, she sprinkles talcum powder over his body, dresses him in ironed clothes, combs his hair, sits him down in the chair, makes the bed with laundered white sheets, and takes him out in his wheelchair. Despite being engaged in unpleasant chores, she appears always bright. She has brought him cologne that smells of champak blooms as a present, and she dabs it in his armpits and on his chest. His eyes close as he sits in the caress of its heady scent.

'I hope the fragrance won't give you a headache?'

'Actually, no. There was a champak tree in the backyard in my teacher's home. This teacher of mine, Joisa was his name. In the early morning, I used to climb that tree like a monkey to pluck a basket of champak flowers for Joisa to use in his puja.'

Memories flash by as he sits back with his eyes closed. Jyothi won't understand, so he doesn't speak aloud. It being the day of fasting on Ekadashi, the eleventh of the month, neither Joisa nor Rukminiamma ate all day. Their shrunken faces were amusing to see. Rukminiamma wouldn't so much as speak to him, for if she did she would be polluted. The following morning, as soon as the gong and conch sounded from the house, he would run to their backyard, the smell of fresh hot dosas hitting his nostrils as he stood out to wait. First, the sizzle of wet batter on the hot griddle. Then, the sizzling would cease, which meant the ritual offering of dosa to the household deity had commenced. In a while, Rukminiamma would appear on the veranda to place a banana leaf on its floor, and smilingly anticipate that Krishnappa would sprint up. She would serve him hot dosas and a peppery chutney made from coconuts that came every month from Krishnappa's home. After eating until his belly was full of dosas, he would discard the banana leaf, wipe the place down with cow dung and water, and wash his hands with the water that Doddamma, keeping a safe distance from him, poured out. Just as he was about to take off for home, Joisa would come out, shivering on account of the wet cotton dhoti on his body, a bunch of sacred tulsi leaves tucked in his tuft of hair, and standing with his eyes closed, facing the east, he would direct Krishnappa to recite the multiplication table for eighteen. Before he could be asked to recite one more, for nineteen, Krishnappa would slip away.

Outdoors in his wheelchair, the warmth of the sun permeates his fragrant body, and he feels good. As he sits there, he remembers Nagaraj's words: 'These are not merely matters of personal morals.' Krishnappa's mind yearns for the pleasure of wandering in the past. The web is spinning around him tightly. Preparations are on for the ceremony to honour him – a scheme that Gowda, Bhatta and Veeranna have hatched. Couldn't it be justified as a historical necessity? As individual good for the sake of the people's good? What will Nagaraj say to this sort of argument? He will probably say that the question is irrelevant. Or that benefit to the class you represent can take all of society forward only so much and no more. It wouldn't be a surprise if you were doing it for your own welfare. The question of what is pure and what is corrupt is irrelevant, he would say. Bhatta and Gowda have profited from the Tenancy Act. In a parliamentary set-up, it is not possible to bring in a system that is favourable to the landless and the working class. Commit yourself to such a system, and you'll find these selfsame Bhattas and Gowdas will eventually turn against you – just as they did when you fought for the tenant farmers. Having defeated the fat feudal landlords, you are now supported by these capitalist landowners who have emerged as the result of your politics. For the wheel to come full circle, you must stand up for those who really work their land. In the present crisis, it may be in their own interest that the capitalist landowning class should oppose the fascism which the neo-colonial power has created. In that case, use them ... This, perhaps, is how Nagaraj would think ... Krishnappa feels dizzy with these formulations. Jyothi is talking of her wedding plans. Shopping for the wedding dresses, the design of the marriage thali she will wear, etc. Krishnappa becomes engrossed in her talk as he sits there being massaged by her.

* * *

Luckily, Gowri arrives after Sita has left for the bank. She comes in a sari, has tied her hair in a simple knot, and carries a handbag that hangs from her shoulder. Nagesh brings her a chair. She introduces herself to Jyothi with a 'hello'. Krishnappa sits quietly, his eyes on her. Last night, he saw only the few greys in her hair. Now, he sees that her face shows some signs of age. The same shining eyes, but with fine wrinkles around them. The body nevertheless lean and firm. Next to Jyothi, she looks the more mature. Since he is at fifty himself, Gowri might be around forty. Her eyes, lively and alert, take in everything, but sleepless nights and the fear of loneliness have taken their toll. At the time of the break-up in America, she must have said unpleasant things out of bitterness. Days and nights spent in striving for professional accomplishment have taken the playfulness from her demeanour.

Gowri lights a cigarette and puts it between Krishnappa's lips, lights another for herself, and asks Jyothi apologetically:

'Does he have your permission to smoke?'

'No. But it's all right this one time,' Jyothi says. She is kneading the soles of Krishnappa's feet with her hands. The presence of another woman seems to have made her somewhat self-conscious.

'Don't you think he could be made to sit in a bathtub?' Gowri asks.

'Hydrotherapy is good for him, but there is no bathtub.'

'Wait a minute! The guest house has a bath. I trained in hydrotherapy in Philadelphia. We can, between the two of us, handle it, can't we?'

Jyothi is quiet, as if she knows it is not her place to reply. Set on putting her idea to work, Gowri goes and talks to Veeranna who is outside in the hall. In the guest house, Krishnappa can rest well. Jyothi can be brought there in the car, in the mornings. After she is done with looking after him in the mornings, Gowri can take over the rest. Veeranna, who is anxious for Krishnappa to recover his health, agrees to the arrangement. Everybody understands the need for Krishnappa to be away from Sita. So it is decided that he will be transferred to the guest house tomorrow morning.

In the afternoon, Krishnappa's mother Sharadamma arrives from the village, brought there by a young man. She is shocked to see a woman smoking as she sits with her son. Addressing his seventy-year-old mother, decked up like a heggadathi in a sari, Krishnappa says, sounding cross:

'Why did it take so long for you to come? What do you do there all alone? Can't you come and stay here with me?'

'Why should I come and cook for you here? Don't you have your wife for that?' she taunts him, with a laugh. Then she goes into the kitchen to make his favourite thondekai palya and curry.

'Avva, Avva,' shouts Krishnappa. But she is busy with the supplies in the kitchen, taking out from the bag and arranging all that she has brought with her – limes, country lemons, chakota, kesavu leaves for patrode and thondekai.

'I'm coming, don't shout!' she says as she comes back into the room holding a bottle of tender mango pickle.

'The cure for this affliction is to have pigeon's blood rubbed on you. According to our Joisa, you get a stroke if a certain bird flies over your head. He, too, told me to have you rubbed with pigeon's blood. By the way, your Doddamma, god bless her, passed away. She didn't take to her bed even for a day. Having had her meal, she came out to the veranda with her basket of cotton wool, and right in the middle of teasing wicks for the oil lamp that they place before the household god, her eyes closed. Now poor Joisa is all alone. She made this before she died. Joisa sent it for you – your favourite pickle.'

Sharadamma wipes her eyes. Krishnappa keeps himself from tears with difficulty. In his weakened state, Krishnappa's control over his emotions has loosened. Now, out of fear that his mother might close her eyes forever with no one near, he says, 'You are not going away. You stay here, with me.'

'What is there for me here?' she says in mock anger. 'There is not even a fistful of soil to grow something anywhere around this house. No, please, I can't be here for more than two days. Besides, what about your paddy field? Don't I have to hold on to it? If I were to lease it, tomorrow the guy will say it is his. Some law – they say it was you who got it made. We have to live with it.'

Not even a fistful of soil – Krishnappa is stung. If it had been the previous house in Gandhi Bazar, she would have liked it better. It was livelier there.

Gowri thrills at the sight of mother and son chattering comfortably about the goings-on of the village. At one point halfway through, the mother remembers that the dishes in the kitchen remain unwashed and becomes uneasy. On noticing this, Gowri goes in to tidy up the kitchen.

'What kind of a woman is she that she smokes bidis?' Sharadamma says.

'Don't you chew tobacco?' asks Krishnappa with a laugh.

'Seems like a good person, though,' she says, and goes back to talking about the village. Which girl had started menstruating, which of the cattle had contracted disease, how bad the mould infestation was in the betel-nut palms this year, who gave birth, in which wedding did the in-laws come to blows ... and on and on ... Suddenly, in mid-flow, she sighs:

'Poor Joisa, some days he doesn't cook for himself. I go over to milk the cow for him. He warms up the milk and drinks it – that's all.'

'How is everyone in uncle's family... ?'

'Ayyo, it's a long story...' and she starts narrating an epic.

When Sita returns from office in the evening, she is pleased to see her daughter in the grandmother's lap. When she sees Gowri seated there as well, she walks away to the kitchen, simmering. 'It's not her fault. Poor thing. You have made her insecure,' Gowri says to Krishnappa. Krishnappa agrees with this, and he is grateful to her for lessening the disquiet in him with her comment. Gowri gets up and says she will talk to Sita and goes to the kitchen.

* * *

'Salaam to Gowdru, salaam! How is our leader's health?'

Abdul Rahman is dear to Krishnappa.

He takes off his topi and bows theatrically, then pulling up a chair, sits down. He is a man of creamy complexion with the genteel manners of the once-wealthy of the old Mysore province. He dresses elegantly in a long coat, his demeanour is cheerful, courteous and without a touch of false modesty. All the old wealth was spent on the high life, and now Rahman is the president of the Bidi Workers' Union. His ample elegance is in evidence even if it is merely tea that is being served to his guests. Krishnappa enjoys his half jokey, half proud boasts of pure Persian ancestry.

The background to their intimacy is this: Three years ago, the Muslims of Chikmagalur threw stones at a passing Ganapati procession for the noise it was creating at prayer time. The reprisal was severe. Muslim dwellings were set on fire. Riots broke out in several parts of the town. Rumours went around that the mosque held a stockpile of firearms. There were many deaths, and right in the heart of town, in broad daylight, a car carrying a Muslim couple and their four children was stopped in the middle of the street, doused with petrol and set ablaze. The Koran burned in the town square.

Glib politicians delivered messages of peace, discipline, brotherhood, while Krishnappa alone went to Chikmagalur and made a statement condemning, in no uncertain terms, the Hindus who had carried out atrocities against Muslims. People were shocked. Death threats came in the mail from everywhere. The men of his party criticized him, called his action stupid – the Muslims voted for the ruling party after all, why lose the Hindu vote? Krishnappa, who was getting soft from the many compromises of political life, once again became taut with vitality. He regained the stern stance of old. He proved to the people of the state that anyone who did not dare to be unpopular could not be a political leader.

Rahman was a party member, vilified, on the one hand, as a liquor-loving lackey of the Hindus by orthodox Muslims, and looked upon, on the other hand, with suspicion by the Hindus. After this episode, he began to think of Krishnappa as his brother.

Today, Rahman sits with his topi in his lap and talks to Krishnappa dispassionately, in soft words, about the political situation in the country. Since the Muslims in the country are largely on the prime minister's side, here in the state, where they favour the party ruling at the centre as well, they are in the camp opposed to the chief minister. In a few days, the CM's party is going to split nationally. It will bring the prime minister's party into majority in the state legislature. The chief minister will not be able to continue without their support. Even with their support, he will be only five clear of the prime minister's group. To maintain this fragile margin, a lot of money will be spent.

'So what do you think we should do, Rahman?'

Rahman winks. 'Veeranna is pouring money into making you the chief minister. Let him spend. After all, it's ill-gotten gains. Be oblivious, turn a blind eye.' He then speaks with seriousness, in English: 'The question before the country is a serious one because the prime minister is on the way to becoming a dictator. Their group, too, is asking for our support. They know that, though ours is a small party, you, Gowdre, have an all-India stature. As they too talk of socialism, a few in our party feel an affinity towards them. But if we support the present chief minister now, since he has already become weak, it is possible to get him to form the cabinet with you, Krishnappa Gowda, as the leader. He will accept this arrangement until the next election. Crafty rogue that he is, he is secretly trying to curry favour with the prime minister's group as well. But his party rival doesn't like this. So the question before us is how we may retain the five members in our camp. In this context, the felicitation ceremony for Krishnappa Gowda is an important strategy. The chief minister will speak on that day. The Assembly will meet shortly after, and everything will have to be decided then. You, Gowdre, should rest. Don't get involved in any of it. If we announce that a government will be formed with Krishnappa Gowda as its leader, chances are some junior legislators – about ten – who have joined the prime minister's group may switch over to our side. That's why this scoundrel chief minister appears willing to approach the governor to tell him that if our party forms the government it will have his support. They have started collecting signatures. Everyone is waiting for the ruling party to break up.'

'I find the whole thing disgusting, Rahman!'

'Can you afford to feel disgusted at this point, Gowdre?' Rahman says, switching from English to Kannada – whenever he wants to appear to talk light-heartedly, he switches to Kannada.

'I doubt whether anything can be achieved at all in such a situation.'

'Our aim, come next election, is to make sure the prime minister's party loses. Or else, they will be firmly in power for the next hundred years. That's why you should become the leader – so that the prime minister's group doesn't get stronger. But Gowdre, what I want to tell you is this: First, as soon as you come to power, you should lower the ceiling on landownership. Second, fix a minimum wage for landless labourers. Then many of those fools who have joined the PM's group will come back to you. This scoundrel CM knows that. He is looking to be the chief himself by using us. Our Veeranna will take care of all that. You don't worry, close your eyes and get well, leave the rest to us. It's crucial that we seize power now. I'll bring Nagaraj around. We want you to remain a great man – untouched by the politics around you.'

'All that is okay, Rahman, but doesn't it mean we would have to include close to thirty or thirty-five rats in the cabinet?'

'Wait, Gowdre. Let the party break up. We'll make the scoundrel CM's men fall at your feet, they'll do what we want them to. All he wants is that his enemy should not be the CM. Shall I take your leave now?'

Rahman presses Krishnappa's hand affectionately.

* * *

Maheshwarayya's face is perfectly calm. Nagesh is excited. Not sure whether Maheshwarayya or he should be the one to spill the beans, he is about to explode.

Maheshwarayya calls out to Sitamma. Coming out of the kitchen, Sitamma says a curt, 'What?'

'This is for you to build the house,' and he puts ten thousand rupees in her hand. Sitamma, who is standing, collapses in the chair, lost for words.

'I won fifty thousand at the races. How am I going to spend the money at my age? I need a place to stay when I am in Bangalore, don't I? It seems you own a site – Nagesh tells me.' To Krishnappa, he says, 'If I try to return the money to Veeranna, he won't take it. That's what Nagesh says. Here, I made out a draft for fifteen thousand as a donation to the hostel he runs.' Maheshwarayya places a demand draft on the table.

'I feel like a smoke. Nagesh, may I have a cigarette?'

Nagesh gives him his Wills. Lighting it, Maheshwarayya asks, 'Where is Gowri? I heard that she has arrived?' Upon turning around, he notices Gowri and greets her, 'Namaskara!' His eyes sparkle on seeing her.

Unable to contain himself, Nagesh pipes up:

'See, Gowdre! He wouldn't listen to me, forced me to accept two thousand rupees. He wants to give your nurse a wedding present, so he has made a draft of two and half thousand for her. He has sent off a cheque for ten thousand rupees he says he had borrowed. He has kept only ten thousand for himself…'

Maheshwarayya stands up on seeing Krishnappa's mother, who is coming out of the kitchen, and says, 'How are you? Well, I hope?'

She lowers herself to sit on the floor, and once more narrates the story of Rukminiamma's earthly departure.

'I've given up gambling on horses,' Maheshwarayya says to Krishnappa. 'I have a small bit of farmland and a shack near Dharwad. I will go and live there.' He puts the draft for Jyothi on the table. He looks tired. Krishnappa knows that he doesn't like his generosity praised.

'Krishnappa, they say there's going to be some ceremony to honour you in your village. You can be sure I will be there a day earlier. All right? Let's go,' he says, and before anyone can react, leaves with Nagesh.

Sita rushes to the door and calls out. Wiping tears from her face she says:

'The money is not important to me. All I want is that he should live so that my thali, my sacred status as a wife, remains intact. I don't want the money. Please, take it back.'

Maheshwarayya senses the sincerity of her words. He says, 'Your husband is a great man. You should let him grow further. My money is his money, there's no difference. Please keep it.'

'What do you know of the difficulty of being a great man's wife? Do you know how people treat me as an inferior?' Sita starts to sob.

Maheshwarayya comes back to where she is standing and says, 'I realize your difficulty. He knows it, too. He will understand, give him some time.'

He gets into the autorickshaw Nagesh has called, and is soon on his way to catch a bus to Dharwad.

* * *

As Sita stands at the door staring after Maheshwarayya, Gowri says to Krishnappa in English:

'What Maheshwarayya did was unfair. He has crushed your wife with his generosity.'

In the moment, Krishnappa does not know what to say.

'It may weigh heavily on her,' he says eventually, 'but I doubt it. She couldn't bring herself to give her mother a sari in appreciation of her help at the time of her confinement. She is a very stingy woman – both in money and in spirit.'

How easily he has maligned his wife to another woman! It shocks Gowri more than it does Krishnappa. She appears quite angry when she says, 'Why do you live with a woman whom you disparage so much? It seems you decided to marry a woman inferior to you just to boost your ego.'

Krishnappa is stunned. As he sits there tongue-tied, Sita, who can't bear to look at their faces when she comes in, carries on hurriedly to the kitchen to help Krishnappa's mother with the food she is making for her son. Gowri gets up to put the girl to sleep.

* * *

The guest house is on Veeranna's farm, about ten miles clear of the city. It is set in a carefully landscaped garden, against a backdrop of dramatic boulders. In the grove are coconut, lemon, orange, pomegranate, sapota, jamun, guava. Grapevines grow over its front. The guest house is a stylish modern structure with a tiled roof, framed on either side by thickets of Chinese bamboo. By the grove of fruiting trees is a swimming pool. For guests who fancy a bit of riding, Veeranna has kept a handsome, well-groomed white horse. In the front of the house, two deer graze in a fenced courtyard. Beyond, in two specially created grottos, peacocks strut. Such is the ambience of the guest house – a satisfying blend of rural serenity and modern amenities has been achieved. Though this is not Krishnappa's first visit, he feels invigorated by its fresh air this time.

He has come with his mother, Nagesh and Gowri Deshpande. Sita's widowed mother has come to stay with her from Tumkur, because Sita will only visit him on days when the bank is closed. Everyone thinks that this arrangement is essential for Krishnappa's peace of mind. Veeranna promises that he will bring the little one at least every other day, after school.

Although he has come here seeking solitude, Krishnappa misses the stream of visitors who came to him every day. Most people came to see him perhaps because he was dying, which made him feel that he was still an important man. Here, there is less of an opportunity for that satisfaction. To his consternation, he realizes that his will to live is nourished on luxuries provided by Veeranna's generosity. The connection between his lifestyle and the corrupt system that provides him not only these amenities but the support of the people is so close. Even as he spurns the position of chief minister – and by doing so, perhaps, further ensures that outcome – the conspiracy to make him the chief minister is relishable, and it brings him new vitality in his declining health. His letter of resignation remains in his pocket. Maheshwarayya's prophecy ticks away in his mind. Does he really wish to become the chief minister by exploiting the present system? Or is the wish to renounce it all, distance himself from the sources of corruption, and in the face of death, once again strive for the good of the people as well as his own inner well-being stronger? Which of the two could be true? He had failed to find a question for the hermit that would have impelled an answer. He finds himself in a similar spot again.

Perhaps it is that these questions are meaningless. There are no real moral dilemmas. It is doubtful that our deepest desires pull equally in opposite directions – 'should I, or should I not?' If the soul is pulled more firmly in one direction, then it is not in a moral dilemma. It faces an impulse. An itch. We wish to look good to ourselves.

With a sigh, he admits the realization that there would have been no question of his being tempted if he had disliked the environment in this retreat. It troubles him. He is certain in his mind that he had not been relying on Nagaraj to ignore his resignation, that he was not being melodramatic when he had left it to Nagaraj to decide what to do with his letter. Once again, Krishnappa is confused about his own thought process.

He asks Nagesh to telephone Veeranna and ask him to stop by, and sitting in the shade of a mango tree, he loses himself in the soft murmur of windblown bamboo.

* * *

His mother, however, is all agog. Watching her run around, with the loose end of her sari tucked in at the waist, Krishnappa can't help but smile at the thought of how pleased she would be if her son were to own such a place. She milks the cow, and covering the pail in the folds of her sari to thwart the evil eye of people or of birds flying over, she stands before Krishnappa and says in a conspiratorial tone, 'Have you seen anything like this before?'

Krishnappa gives her a quizzical look.

'There is at least another bucket of milk in that cow's udders. My hands got tired, so the servant is milking her.'

She shows him the frothy milk just for a second and covers it again.

'I'll warm it up and you can drink it then. Do you remember, you used to put your mouth to the udders of our cow Kaveri? What a gentle animal! Never kicked at you even once. It's one of her offspring that I am milking these days. At the most, she gives a seer of milk, half of which I give Joisa – so that the brahmin may pour it over the head of the idol…'

Gowri comes out after her bath wearing trousers and a jubba, and sits at a distance drying her hair in the sun. Seeing her lighting a cigarette, Krishnappa's mother makes a face. Krishnappa says, smiling:

'And your tobacco?'

'Whatever I brought with me is finished. Tell Nagesh to get some more,' she says cheerfully enough, and calls out to Gowri.

'I have made some kadubu. Come in and eat it.'

She had left some of last night's batter for her daughter-in-law in the house in Sadashivanagar, and brought the rest with her in the car in the morning. Now, she cooks it in banana leaves and serves it with coconut chutney. She serves the favourite tender mango pickle with its sauce, that Rukminiamma had made just before she died.

'Can you tell which tree the mangoes came from?' she asks her son. Krishnappa tries to remember the trees he knew. There was one by the stream in Huliyooru, one on the hill above Joisa's house, another one by the fence down the hill where he used to graze the cattle – that loose fence gave him a lot of trouble in keeping the cattle from straying. The three trees yielded the best mangos for pickling. You snapped the stem, and the aroma would hit your nostrils. The fruit was hard when you squeezed it, crunchy when you bit it. The pickles from those mangoes stayed three years and even longer. Each of the three mangos was distinct in flavour, in the way it took spice, in the way it cured. His mother waits eagerly for his answer, her wrinkled face pickled with mischief. Krishnappa bites into the piece twice, and says with some uncertainty, 'The one near the stream?'

She beams with delight.

Veeranna comes in the afternoon. 'You sent for me?'

Krishnappa asks him to take a seat. Pushing a cigarette between his lips, he asks him to light it. Veeranna does not miss the agitation on Krishnappa's face. He waits patiently for him to begin.

'Mr Veeranna, I want to ask you something. Kindly don't misunderstand me.'

'Please ask, Gowdre.'

'How much money are you spending to make me the chief minister?'

'Gowdre, I know that you are a man of very strict principles. But I also know that you are a smart man. When one enters politics, one should accept these inevitabilities.'

'I know that, but it is not my kind of politics.'

'I know that as well, Gowdre. But we have a crisis in our country. There's no other way to stop the dictatorship from advancing. You can practise your politics when the danger has passed.'

'Should I assume that you have no selfish motive?'

Veeranna looks hurt.

'Gowdre, if there's one thing in you, it's your suspicious nature. I've heard people complain that you are like the banyan: you don't let anyone near you grow. But I also know that those close to you don't have your ability.'

'You didn't answer my question.'

'Okay, Gowdre, after all I am a businessman. Do you want me to give up my businessman's dharma?'

'But people didn't elect me to help you play *your* dharma.'

'Ayyo, my god! I don't understand you. I am human, am I not? I too have my pride, don't I? I wish to see you in that chief minister's chair at least for a year. You don't have to do anything for me. I swear, I won't come to you for a single favour. Doesn't the rascal who is the CM now do what I ask him to do for me already?'

Krishnappa had thought that Veeranna would stalk off hurt, but he was wrong. Veeranna keeps up his smooth talk. Being a skilled politician, Krishnappa decides to test Veeranna.

'While I am the CM,' he says, 'you will get no contracts.'

'Fine, I won't,' says Veeranna calmly. 'Don't I know that you are not someone who does that sort of thing? I have made my fortune, Gowdre. Now, it makes me happy just to put a great man like you in that seat, that's all. But it makes me sad that you don't understand this and are being petty.'

'You see, my health is bad. I sometimes wonder whether I am not using my illness to gain the sympathy of others.'

'Come on, Gowdre! Now listen: as you will have to share power with that rascal, you won't be able to accomplish everything you mean to at present. But you might accomplish one or two things. You are a seasoned politician. You should sit and talk with the others and pursue what is possible for the time being, and gain your strength by the next election.'

'Do you believe that ten legislators might cross over to our side if I were the leader?'

'If it were not so, would our rascal CM have proposed your name? Even now, he is secretly trying to align himself with the prime minister.'

Krishnappa puts out the cigarette. Veeranna gets up to leave.

'Do you believe me now? I'm taking your leave. Let me know if you need anything.'

After the conversation is over, Krishnappa remains in good spirits generally. He does not talk about it any more. When Jyothi comes the next morning, Gowri helps her put him in the bathtub, where in the warm water he is pleased to find he can move his afflicted limbs without much difficulty. Trained in hydrotherapy herself, Gowri sends Jyothi away. From then on, Jyothi comes out only to assist him with his morning excretory functions.

Gowri smiles when Krishnappa, out of shyness, won't remove his underwear in front of her. The next morning, he gives in and allows her his undershirt.

When Gowri's hands start moving over his hands and legs, the touch doesn't feel just clinical. She seems to have wanted to touch him, which brings a thrill and warmth to Krishnappa's body. This is the first time he has felt this way since he became ill, and he is puzzled by it.

Gowri helps Krishnappa out of the tub and takes him to the garden in his wheelchair. He is more at ease when she is in trousers and jubbas, so that is what she mostly wears now, and ties her hair into a knot with a scarf. She sets him up in the garden and helps him with his exercises, and reads her favourite novels to him. Krishnappa may paint vivid pictures for her with tales of his cow-herding days, describing not least the birds that visited the peepul tree which spread above him. His mother, too, whenever she is free from her morning chores, will sit with them. Once, when Gowri has gone inside for something, she asks, 'Why didn't you marry her?'

Krishnappa is taken aback. His mother persists. She says, naively: 'In our family, quite a few men have had two wives. Why not you?'

'Please, Amma, don't ever talk about such things in front of Gowri!' Krishnappa huffs.

'Why would I talk? Aren't you a grown-up man? Instead of wasting away like this, I said why not make her your wife? That's all.'

He is touched by his mother's straightforwardness. Gowri has a life of her own, however, and he is mindful not to let his thoughts run any further in that direction.

He is able to squeeze the rubber ball with his fingers. He can even move his leg slowly. Gowri says that, within a month, he should be able to walk on crutches. Her vacation is only for one month. Gowri has noticed that the thought of her going away makes Krishnappa anxious, so she doesn't bring it up.

The days have been pleasant and comfortable. At night, the stars appear bright and clear, ornaments in a blue sky. At times, when Gowri and Krishnappa are in deep conversation, the peacocks dance, opening their plumage wide like an umbrella, aquiver as if possessed. Mother talks only about cows, milk and fruits, and complains at least once a day that no jackfruit is available for jackfruit kadubu, making Krishnappa's mouth water. Nagesh sits at the table, engaged seriously in his authorship of Krishnappa's biography. Occasionally, he reads out what he has written, making Krishnappa squirm.

Krishnappa often rehearses what he would like to say to Gowri in one or two pithy sentences. 'Gowri, I had been in love with you. But after the hellish experience I had in the Warangal jail, I couldn't bring myself to ask you to marry me.' At these times, he lapses into silence, thinking that the words don't really say anything. Though she is approaching middle age, she appears to him, once again, like a bloom of closed petals. With time, gradually, they stop talking about their past days.

One day, Krishnappa is sitting quietly by the bamboo. Gowri, too, sits nearby, reading something. His mother is in the kitchen, making savoury patrode. All of a sudden, Krishnappa starts a song. Looking up in surprise, Gowri sees him singing with his eyes closed. His serene face, his hair and beard with hints of grey in them, they make her happy. She plucks the blades of green grass and the tiny flowers that grow around her. When Krishnappa stops, she starts – singing his favourite Kabir songs softly.

Another day, she stops Krishnappa's wheelchair by the side of the swimming pool, takes off her clothes and stands just in her bikini. He is flustered by the casualness of her undressing like that. Standing on the jumping board on high, she stretches her arms and straightens her taut body briefly like an arrow about to be shot, and plunges into the pool, disappearing into the water and reappearing gradually – her dark hair, back, her narrow waist, ample hips and dainty feet become visible while she moves in the water. In his imagination, Krishnappa's whole body moves in unison with hers. Krishnappa, who had been an expert swimmer in his younger days, becomes one with her in her breaststrokes and the kicks of her legs. For a moment, he forgets that half of his body is inert. Coming out of the water, Gowri walks towards him. Drops of water glisten on her smooth, taut skin. Water trickles down from her hair. Feeling the coolness of her body as if it is his own, he shivers. He fears that her vibrant body may recoil from his sluggish body, and closes his eyes in envy. But his eyes open in surprise when he realizes that her wet hands are caressing his cheeks and neck. 'Do you feel like sitting in the bathtub?' she asks. He feels thrilled because she has addressed him in the singular form, in the intimate manner. Still in her bikini, she wheels him into the room and closes the door. She fills the huge bathtub with warm water and undresses Krishnappa. In a deep voice which he hasn't heard until now, she says, 'I'm going undress you completely,' and starts pulling down his briefs. Krishnappa, in fear, is about to stop her but feels helpless. When she does not show any revulsion for the nakedness of his sickly body, he feels grateful towards her. It seems her eyes, in their excited state, don't notice anything. Leaning his body against her own skilfully, she lifts him and eases him into the water. She then gets into the tub herself, removes her bikini and tosses it away. Her body embraces his – both having become light in the water. Krishnappa's eyes become misty with tears.

Gowri, who held him in her embrace for quite some time, gets up and spreads soft white towels on the floor. Lifting Krishnappa up and laying him on the towels, she too lies down next to him, hugging him. With her lips, breasts and thighs, she presses herself to him.

'I can't now, Gowri,' he says in despair, in a deep voice that seems not his.

Gowri is silent like a well. She is like the earth that holds the sprouting seed within its warm, dark recesses, patiently. Her fingers play on his whole body as though it were a musical instrument. They search the nooks and corners of his body as if they were founts waiting to be awakened. Her eyes close as if in meditation. She slithers over his body, her moist, warm vagina softly rubbing his belly, thighs, sides, arms and cheeks. Her lips, nibbling pleasingly from the top, move downwards. Her breath tickles the recesses of his body, making him rejoice in the fact that he possesses eyes, ears, neck, stomach and penis. As his body warms up, sprouting and springing, and he lies on his back with his limbs splayed, she straddles him and lets his erection enter her. Like the opening strains of a musical piece, her movements are slow. Tears flow from Krishnappa's eyes. 'Amma!' he utters. Gowri bends down and lowers herself lightly on his body. Krishnappa falls into a deep sleep. Upon waking up, he wonders whether he was dreaming and notices that he is lying on a towel and Gowri is sitting next to him, naked, smoking a cigarette. He looks at her face. Is it out of pity that she has treated him so? He is not sure.

His mother has the room adjoining his. In the evening, as Gowri and Krishnappa are feeding the deer nibbles of grass with their hands, she comes out and tells them that she will sleep in Gowri's room and that Gowri should switch with hers. Without waiting for an answer, she leaves. Krishnappa looks at Gowri with a smile on his face.

At night, Gowri sleeps by Krishnappa's side. In the warmth of her body, he falls asleep soundly. In the morning, when she arrives, Jyothi senses a change in Krishnappa.

* * *

As everyone has expected, the ruling party splits nationwide. Rahman and Nagaraj come to see Krishnappa. Nagaraj looks worried. In view of the prime minister's proclivities, he takes the position now that it is all right to extend limited support to the chief minister. The breakaway faction has petitioned the governor to allow the formation of a new government under its leadership. After making a rather complex calculation for an hour, Rahman's figures yield up five more for their party. And yet, Chandrayya of the prime minister's side has made a statement that many from the chief minister's faction have already joined them. Newspapers carry one set of statements on one page, counterstatements on another, sowing confusion everywhere.

Nagaraj has brought with him a prepared statement for Krishnappa to sign. He reads it aloud with a feeling of nausea. The statement says that their party will support the present government. Krishnappa signs it. Rahman says:

'Five more from the CM's group may yet join the other side. To get people from their side to join us, we will have to make you the chief minister. We'll have to wait and see.'

'Disgusting!' says Nagaraj and lights a Charminar. 'There's anarchy in the country. According to the news reports, people are dying of cholera in Raichur district. Every day there comes news of looting, women being raped. And here we are, still engaged in the farce of forming a new cabinet.'

Rahman is not interested in this kind of political discourse. He is already dreaming of becoming the transport minister in Krishnappa's cabinet.

The day after Krishnappa's statement is published, the tabloid daily *Kidi* publishes a story on Krishnappa. He has steeped himself in debauchery on Veeranna's farm, it says, has become a total slave to corruption. The country is burning, but here Veeranna has provided Krishnappa with a call girl from Delhi for his pleasure. It chastises Krishnappa, once a revolutionary, on trading his moral scruples for medical treatment. The paper comes to Krishnappa by registered mail. He tells Nagesh to burn it before Gowri can come across it.

Krishnappa tries to forget his troubles in the embrace of Gowri's naked body. He feels he cannot turn back, no matter how hard he tries. He can hardly immerse himself in the present political morass either. He is disgusted by the announcements – one day defections, the next day their denials – published every day in the dailies. Veeranna has not been coming to the farm often, being preoccupied with these ins and outs, but the people of his political group visit frequently. With the exception of Nagaraj, everyone sings his praises more than ever. Hereafter, Krishnappa is convinced, it will be impossible for him to have a single genuine friend. Lamenting privately that his personal life is now over, he lies down and surrenders his body to Gowri's touch. Gowri, on the other hand, grows in cheer. When she is elsewhere on the farm, strolling, quiet, Krishnappa's mind still dwells on her. In the deep layers of her mind, she will preserve his purity and save him. But she, who can protect the jewel of his soul, must return to Delhi, must live her life. She may not desire me as much as I do her. My body is a cracked vessel. Such miseries crowd his mind. He tells himself that he should retire from this dirty politics, send in a letter of resignation, return to his village. His wish is really for that peepul tree in the timeless afternoon. Oh, to listen to cowbells tinkling against the background murmur of the running stream, and to watch the birds descend on the guava tree in front. In a state of repose like that, he would love to catch a glimpse, as long ago, of the rare golden-winged bird with the long tail. But what is past doesn't come back, and he is aware of the clash of desire and reality.

Meanwhile, one day, who should show up but his old school friend Hanumanayaka. Krishnappa is listening to his daughter's chatter when Hanumanayaka comes in.

'Where were you all this time, you pig?' Krishnappa says, taking him to task. Hanumanayaka offers him the cane he has brought, and stands bowing low theatrically.

'Please accept this cane which this servant of yours personally cut and shaped,' he says, and with a flourish leans his crooked self on the cane.

'Our leader is not able to walk like this any more,' he says, walking straight and stylish. 'So he will have to walk this way,' and saying so, he limps with the cane in his hand.

When Gowri comes in, in her trousers, he bites his tongue and becomes serious. Krishnappa bursts into laughter. Gowri has never seen him laugh like this before. Hearing Hanumanayaka's voice, Krishnappa's mother comes out.

'Where have you been, you drifter?' she says. 'If I knew you were coming, I would have asked you to bring some sour plum. How is everyone in our village? What have you been up to these days? Matchmaking, as usual?' From her pouch, she extracts tobacco and betel nut, gives Hanumanayaka a share, and starts spreading lime on a betel leaf for herself.

Hanumanayaka, who had saved him from drowning in the river – whenever this Hanumanayaka comes to see him, Krishnappa becomes his boyhood self again. He is a wandering soul, no mother, father, brother or sister to call his own. The rogue had dropped out of school to join the Bhagavata drama troupe, where he retained the clown's part. Yesterday is behind him, and tomorrow hasn't come yet. Where he is today, that's his dwelling. It doesn't matter whose home it is, announcing 'Here I am!' he makes straight for the kitchen, strikes up a conversation with the women and makes them laugh. From place to place he goes, participating with matchmaking women in the enterprise to decide which marriageable girl might be suitable for which marriageable young man. Before a family can properly launch its search, this roving ambassador will have learned its preferences and passed them on. From the kitchen to the bathing place, from there to the spread of betel nuts curing in the open, he will entertain the children with his imitation of a dog's bark and a cat's meow or the groaning of a lorry climbing a slope. Once, in the company of another prankster like himself, he got into a farting contest – getting one coconut for each fart. He was believed to have earned one hundred coconuts. It was not until much later that the loser in the contest learned that the source of Hanumanayaka's farts had been not his rear but his mouth. If he can get some country liquor or arrack on an evening, he is content. After the evening's meal, he will entertain people with his imitation of the way some villagers speak. Everywhere he goes, he takes his smorgasbord of antics for the womenfolk and the children to feast on. A birth, a death, or a wedding – whatever the occasion, Hanumanayaka will be there without fail.

'This is the Hanumanayaka I have told you about,' Krishnappa says, introducing him to Gowri. 'Hanuma the monkey, in act as in name.' Once he is sure that he is among friends, the monkey uncoils his tail to reveal the flame at its tip.

Into their midst he brings Narasimha Bhatta, strutting about in his serge coat, his fat belly sticking out, appearing very busy at the preparations for Krishnappa's felicitation ceremony. How Narasimha Bhatta must have looked when dung water landed on his face. Getting Bhatta's buck-toothed face perfectly and matching his voice, he praises Krishnappa to the skies. For Krishnappa, it is too much to watch, and he laughs as if his sides will split.

For Gowri's benefit he has a serious-looking profile of Krishnappa. Nagesh and Gowri start laughing. He produces, then, the scene when Krishnappa, about to drown, flailed and gurgled: 'I'm drowning! Goodbye, my friend!' For the little girl in his audience who is watching him wide-eyed, he enacts a cat fight.

'What's this, Hanuma! Your whiskers have turned grey and you still haven't stopped your monkeying around?' chides Krishnappa's mother, who has come out of the kitchen to announce that food is ready. Gowri moves to push Krishnappa's wheelchair, and Hanumanayaka watches this 'palanquin-ride' in the pose of a village idiot.

'Now, now, there's no need for that, don't overdo it,' Mother says with a smile, and as she serves him food on his plate, presses him for more news of their village. He has heard the poor are delighted that

Krishnappa will be felicitated, and he has a part in the play *Krishna Sadhana* that is going to be staged on the occasion, and so on. He catches the way Gowri is feeding Krishnappa, each morsel of rice held delicately between the fingertips. Nagesh notices the imitation first, then Gowri sees it too and starts laughing.

* * *

It does not last long. The cheer of Hanumanayaka's visit evaporates the next day when news comes in the papers of a horrible death, which changes everything politically, besides presenting Krishnappa with a moral dilemma.

Before reading the newspapers, Krishnappa was sitting by the bamboo, basking in the morning sun. Jyothi had the day off work and she was relaxing and talking with Gowri about her forthcoming wedding. Hanumanayaka was carving a wooden top for the little girl while recalling a protest from the days of the Quit India Movement of 1942. One day, the schoolboys lay down at the school gate, so that when the headmaster, a man with a Hitler moustache, walked in with his daughter who was a student at the school, they were forced to step over the prostrate boys. Hanumanayaka acted out how he had sneaked a peek up the girl's skirt. Krishnappa was still laughing at the jape when Nagesh came out to give him the newspaper.

Chandrayya had a statement about a pretty girl who worked in a bank, who was returning from a movie she had gone to see after work when a police van drove up and stopped her. Suspicious on seeing a girl walking alone at that hour, the officer questioned her, put her in the van and drove away. Two young gallants turned up to stand guarantee, and took the grateful girl away in their car. They took her crying to a hotel. She begged them to take her home. The young men were important, and telling her that they were so-and-so and so-and-so, urged her to submit to them. Though her father was no more than a retired schoolteacher, though she was poor, the girl did not yield to the enticements they offered her. The young men then locked the room and raped her. Afterwards, they dropped her off at the corner of the street where she lived. Her father demanded to know why she was so late, but no matter how much he scolded her, she wouldn't say. In the morning, she was found dead. She had swallowed Folidol. In her suicide note, she had left a guarded account of her ordeal and said that she was taking her life in order to the preserve the marriage prospects of her sisters.

That was the gist of the report. But the suicide note raised several questions. The father claimed that the police had taken it away, while the police claimed that no such note existed. The police denied that the girl had been in their custody, precluding the chance of any young men coming to the station to secure her release. In his statement, Chandrayya, the leader of the pro-PM group, said that he had learnt from the stricken father that the young men were the CM's son and Veeranna's son. This is what Lalita, the dead girl, had committed to her note. According to the statement, the CM's son had managed to get his hands on the note. In addition to this, Chandrayya's statement said, the blue Fiat they had used was registered to Krishnappa Gowda.

'Nagesh, get me Rahman and Nagaraj. Now,' Krishnappa says. His throat has become dry. Gowri anxiously asks him what is wrong. He gives her the paper. When she finishes reading, he says:

'I had some desire to become the chief minister until I read this. It had revived in me a desire to live. Now, I feel I don't want anything.'

'Isn't it possible that Chandrayya is lying?'

She says that to console him, he knows, for Gowri has not been very enthusiastic for him to become CM. He shakes his head, he doesn't want to be consoled. He feels intensely, in that moment, the helplessness with which he had gone on and on kicking the door and exhausted himself that day in the Warangal jail.

Gowri stands by, chewing the blade of grass she holds in her fingers. In the changed atmosphere, Hanumanayaka stands confused, the top he was carving still in his hand.

* * *

Rahman and Nagaraj arrive. Only Rahman speaks. Nagaraj sits smoking, pressing his forehead. Rahman had gone to see both the chief minister and Veeranna. Both had said their sons were innocent. Rahman had his doubts. Anyway, it is irrelevant whether they are or not. What is important right now is Chandrayya and the political ends to which he is putting the event, stirring up commotion everywhere in the state to force the governor to dismiss the government. Once that is done, the governor, who is the prime minister's puppet anyway, has a splendid chance to suspend the Legislative Assembly. The conditions will be right for mass defections over to their side. On the basis of this incident, five of these swine are about to announce that they are leaving for Chandrayya's group. It's been on the news. The chief minister is trying hard to hold on to his chair at any cost, but he realizes it will be difficult. He knows that Rahman has been planning to organize youth demonstrations throughout the state to demand that Krishnappa Gowda be made the chief minister. Veeranna is going around with the purpose of accomplishing the same. That's why he is not currently in Bangalore. There are six Muslim MLAs on Chandrayya's side. The chief among them wants to be the transport minister. Rahman has gone to him and told him: 'You be the transport minister. I don't want it.' That man has great respect for Gowdru. If he brings the five others who are on his side to us, we will be in the majority. By tomorrow, we will persuade our 'rogue' to resign as CM and propose your name – and so on.

Nagaraj says, 'College students have begun a strike to demand the chief minister's resignation. The law and order situation is rapidly deteriorating. The boys have been stoning police stations. This may very well result in the police opening fire.'

Krishnappa asks Nagaraj, 'Supposing it is true that Veeranna's son and the chief minister's son did such a thing with the help of the police ... ?'

'That's irrelevant, Gowdre. Let's assume they did it. Chandrayya's son, too, could have done it. Aren't the police for protecting those in power? What's so surprising about that?'

Krishnappa becomes angry. 'You talk like a cynic, Nagaraj! Does everything we touch have to be politicized? How disgusting!'

'No, I am speaking of objective reality: the police exist to guard the system. Rapes, robberies, black marketeering are natural elements of the system.'

'Then why do we seek to be in power?'

'Didn't I say earlier that I have my doubts? I still have illusions of being able to stop the system from becoming totally fascist. That's why I support you.'

'Do you think it is possible to keep in check the police atrocities going on now?'

'Maybe, to some extent. But you can't change the character of the class itself.'

Krishnappa gets irritated. Rahman, who is plainly bored, reads the newspaper. Nagaraj excitedly lights another cigarette.

'The state will not disappear until class is totally eradicated. The state needs the police ...'

'Does it mean that the girl's getting murdered, feeling sad about it, protesting it ...'

Krishnappa is unable to finish the sentence. Seeing how emotional he has become, Nagaraj says gently:

'Yes, we should protest. But the reality of parliamentary politics is such that our protest now will only strengthen Chandrayya's hands. The system, while it does the business of killing, also exploits the protest against it.' Becoming emotional himself, he goes on, 'In spite of all this being true, I'm with you because you feel for the dalits and you believe in being able to do something about it right now...'

'To me, love is important. Without love, what kind of revolution can you make? Of what use is revolution then?'

The words burst out of his mouth. In mind and body, he trembles with unease that these words which had overtaken him may sound casual and mundane. His anxiety must have touched Nagaraj, for he falls silent.

* * *

Gowri's heart leaps to her mouth when she sees that Krishnappa is rigid, as though completely paralysed. She brings him down from the chair on to the floor. She makes him crawl in the way he has been taught to do lately. Physical exercise will alert the body. Krishnappa crawls all over the hall like a baby. With the cane he has got from Hanumanayaka in his left hand, he pushes the ball, creating a game for himself. Gowri seems to be lost in thought. On Krishnappa's urging, she says:

'I think I want to talk to your wife.'

'What do you want to talk to her about?'

'Don't you think we are deceiving her?'

'I've felt it, at times. But it's not something I feel very deeply.'

Gowri mulls over this.

'I want you. But my job is in Delhi. I'm very confused.'

'Gowri, I can't ask you for more than what you have given me. I may die any day.'

'But Sita needs you, doesn't she?'

'She does. She, too, has served me – in her view, quite well.'

'But it seems you are destroying each other.'

Gowri utters just what Krishnappa has been thinking.

'Yes. But I feel I am destroying her more.'

It is Gowri's company that has made it possible for him to say as much, and he looks at her face tenderly. It seems she is not thinking about herself. As if to know the harsh truth, she asks:

'Then what do you think is the right thing to do?'

'Look, Gowri, I've learnt to crawl like a baby. I will next learn to limp with the help of this cane. Everything will have to start all over again. Once again, I'll go and sit under that tree – from where Maheshwarayya first picked me up.'

Gowri laughs sadly.

'You think you are a free man, don't you? But you've become a tool of today's politics, that's all,' she says, pressing his leg.

Wondering if she is still thinking about talking to Sita, Krishnappa says, 'Without violence, Gowri, nothing can be achieved.'

'True.' Continuing in a sad voice, she says, 'Should I go once my leave is over? I'll return whenever you need me…' Krishnappa thinks that she has spoken as if she doesn't understand his needs. He detects in her words an appeal to him to explain himself.

'I feel, Gowri, that we will never live as our whole selves.' Krishnappa struggles to express his present predicament. Touching his chest to mean his heart, he says: 'Even here, I am not able to keep my integrity.' He swings his hand to suggest the political world outside and says, 'Not there either.' He sighs softly, and continues, 'All I can do, at the moment, is to try to stand up by leaning on this cane.'

Gowri sits with her head on her folded knees. Krishnappa rests the cane on his thighs, and pressing down on his right hand with all his weight, says:

'I have two wishes. I want to sit under the peepul tree and feel the eternal time. I want again the wonder that I felt when I saw that bird which made its rare appearance. While tending the cattle, I used to run after that bird. Now seen, now not – it used to flit from tree to tree in the forest. Even as I chased, it would disappear. Now, I don't feel like chasing it – it is not possible either. But I want to wait for it. I can speak about this wish of mine to only you and Maheshwarayya. I have yet another wish, though, really, it is not a different wish. I am not sure how to speak of it convincingly. There are those who have reached the shore. The politics of our country has been for the benefit of these people. While that is so, what I have come to realize is that it is not possible to be free from meanness. I would discuss this matter with Annaji: How can our daily lives be made luminous? Isn't it likely that if we should succeed in provoking to anger and indignation those who, in the historical process, have been left to flounder, their anger may burn away society's meanness?'

He is surprised that the words have come out of him so spontaneously. He sees, reflected in Gowri too, his desire to believe mingled with the anxiety of whether it is possible to believe, and Krishnappa realizes talk is needed no more.

He takes from his pocket his letter of resignation, and giving it to her, says, 'Please go out and mail this. And if you could phone Rahman to send for our MLAs.'

Nagesh is told to bring Sita from the bank for an urgent conversation.

With this, he crawls away, pushing the ball with the cane.

Afterword
The Hypocrisy of Great Men

PRAYAAG AKBAR

Avasthe begins at breakneck, even bewildering pace. We meet Krishnappa Gowda ailing, paralysed on his bed, but immediately we are taken to his childhood, to a time of vitality and strength, he is swimming with his friend in the river that runs by his village, the river is in spate, he has swum this flood many times yet suddenly he is beaten, he goes halfway and no more. Another moment of paralysis. His friend dives into the murk and pulls him to the shore. This is the work of the first few lines of this powerful novel. In the next paragraph, slightly older but still a boy, Gowda is flinging a watchmaker's glass case to the ground in a fit of rage, furious at an insult to his honour.

Memory arrives in this fashion in *Avasthe*, fragments colliding, nesting into the other, recollections of bravado, foolhardiness, triumph, desire, uncoiling with such rapidity that you feel at a loss until the distinctive style begins to work upon you and the fragments begin to aggregate. The shattered glass case finds once again its wholeness. The question is: Why shatter it this way? Why tell this remarkable story as this birdshot of scattered memory?

The narrative device U.R. Ananthamurthy uses to enable his chosen method: Krishnappa Gowda, restless revolutionary, shudra, leader of a famous farmer's agitation, political doyen though not yet fifty, has been immobilized. Stuck in his bed, he is thinking back on his life and relating it to his factotum, Nagesh. It does not matter what Nagesh or, presumably, the reader, makes of the narration. For Krishnappa it is a 'means of making sense of his present state'. A plausible reason, certainly, and it allows Ananthamurthy to render in prose the manner in which memory works, inside us and upon us. In these frenetic first pages, we meet the principals of Krishnappa's childhood, his wife, suffering in their loveless marriage and only too capable of inflicting suffering, we encounter Gowri, his life's presiding love, we see the caste battles in college that fired his politics. We even see Gowda descend into a religious fervour that begins with him slicing off a little toe. Apparently unperturbed, he seats himself in front of a holy fire and recites brahmin verses for three days straight, to the horror of his low-caste family, until he ends up walking the streets of his cousin's village naked.

This distinctive narrative style makes for long devastations and fleeting triumphs (as both these live, perhaps, in our memory) yet it did seem also unnaturally rushed. One of Ananthamurthy's skills is the ability to render his characters real at tremendous speed, with insight that leaves you gasping. It also tantalizes – certainly they live and breathe, the people of this story, but we do not get, at first, enough time with Gowri, with Krishnappa's mother, with his first teacher, Maheshwarayya, a fascinating character upon whom other storytellers might have spent ponderous stretches. And then, all of a sudden, it becomes clear why Ananthamurthy is telling this story this way.

We are with Krishnappa in Warangal jail, the site of his second birth, his revolutionary resurrection. He is trapped in a windowless room. His political guru, Annaji, has been murdered by the cops who roam the station's halls. Dust and must, unbearable heat. Two bowls in a corner. 'The two vessels are for two different uses,' the policeman calls out, laughing. We are already in a memory; remember, in the real-time of this novel, Krishnappa is helpless on his bed. He is interrogated, politely at first, then tortured horribly. He shuts his eyes and thinks back to jail cells of his past, during the Mysore Liberation Movement of 1947 and the Quit India Movement of 1942. Torture is resumed, prolonged. He retreats further into memory. He goes to his childhood, his days as a cowherd, resting under a jackfruit tree as the cattle graze. His mother arrives, gives him her share of jackfruit kadubu. And then he is thinking back to Joisa, the teacher at his primary school, and his wife Rukminiamma, so fond of Krishnappa she would feed him little snacks. Yet Rukminiamma, we learn, 'observed the customs of ritual purity to the last degree'. She drops these snacks from above into his outstretched palms. She obsesses about the young shudra boy touching her saris as they dry on the fence before the house. When he misbehaves still, defiant, they laugh together because if she beat him he would be left with welts, but she would suffer from mailige (ritual impurity). In Ananthamurthy's hands, this memory is warm, soft, a retreat for Krishnappa at a time when he is enduring horrifying hardship. Yet it is the juxtaposition of the two that is remarkable – a memory of caste humiliation, rendered pleasant but remembered just when he is being tortured by the police, that age-old institution of landlords and ministers, nizams and colonials. Ananthamurthy is so very subtle, but you feel in your bones the parallel between the two institutions – the soft mortifications that caste occasions as a social structure, and the hard injustice meted out to the lower castes by the instrument of their oppression, India's policemen.

This novel was first published in 1978 and is based loosely on the life of Shantaveri Gopala Gowda. An adherent of Ram Manohar Lohia, Gowda was beloved of the farmers of Karnataka for the Kagodu Satyagraha, an indefinite fast that led to important legislative change. Reading *Avasthe* amid the escalating disturbances of 2020, we seem at once so far and so close to the political world it describes. In *Avasthe,* Krishnappa's body has betrayed him but his political cohort, his herd, needs him more than ever: the unnamed prime minister (clearly Indira Gandhi) and her party, a personality cult that is running roughshod over democratic principles and electoral competition, must not be allowed to take power in Karnataka. Krishnappa is cast as the leader with the moral and political capital to combat the steamrolling national party. Yet Krishnappa has been forged in revolutionary fires, and he spends much of the latter part of the novel contemplating the choice at his hands: should he assume the post of chief minister when he must accept, if he does, that a measure of corruption is inevitable, indeed is part of political life? That the small favours he takes now are part of a systemic venality? Can he head a structure in which rewards are doled out and favours claimed? Or should he stay true to his principles, fight for injustice as he always has, from outside? As underlings in the party conduct the grubbing exercise of counting legislators – a perennial of Indian democratic politics, it seems, longer-serving than any ideology or persona – Krishnappa retreats with Gowri and his mother to a farmhouse owned by one of his supplicants and contemplates the choices before him.

It is reminiscent of the central dilemma of Ananthamurthy's first novel, the celebrated *Samskara* (1965). There Ananthamurthy investigates the proscriptions incumbent on the brahmin, particularly the sexual; here he puts to test the ideals of the revolutionary. There is a great deal of soul-searching in both novels, but we can see, towards the end of *Avasthe*, Ananthamurthy's maturing ideas about human nature: 'Perhaps it is that these questions are meaningless. There are no real moral dilemmas. It is doubtful that our deepest desires pull equally in opposite directions – "should I, or should I not?" If the soul is pulled more firmly in one direction, then it is not in a moral dilemma. It faces an impulse. An itch. We wish to look good to ourselves.'

Avasthe teems with memorable characters. The three women in Krishnappa Gowda's life are remarkable in their own ways. Sita, his wife, seems to fulfil one expression of the old feminine ideal: in Gowda's enfeebled stasis she is the one who cleans his shit and helps him pee, suffering, still, occasional physical abuse and his continuing talk of the other women he has loved. Gowri, his 'milk-complexioned' college mate (in contrast to Krishnappa's 'African prince'), is the woman our protagonist deifies, elevating her to such a standard that for most of their lives the relationship remains chaste. And finally there is Lucina, sexual prey of a rich businessman's son, whom Krishnappa rescues and soon finds himself in bed with. Lucina is the destroyer of inhibition – with her he discovers appetites and freedoms he had so far been unable to access.

Their roles in the novel would seem schematic were it not for Ananthamurthy's skill in making his characters round, fleshed-out: real. Lucina serves as the sexual liberator but Krishnappa is a defender not of her morality but her agency – she laughs when he asks her to marry him. Gowri, paragon of beauty and intellect, is not the blushing virgin of classic understanding. Early in the novel she causes a furore in Krishnappa's hostel when she waits for him in his room. Her mother is the mistress of a rich local businessman and mother and daughter live, in style, under his patronage. When she returns to India, late in the novel, to teach at Miranda House, fresh from a broken relationship with an American academic, she seems somewhat contemptuous – or perhaps only uncaring – of Sita, the bank clerk wife.

Sita herself is no silent sufferer. Though we never see quite why, it is clear she causes Krishnappa a great deal of anguish. She inflicts upon their daughter (whom Krishnappa has cruelly named Gowri) serious physical abuse herself. She is also a reminder of Krishnappa's hypocrisy. Early in the novel, after Krishnappa beats her, she says: 'He thinks he's a big leader! He wants to make a revolution! First let him stop beating his wife, then we'll see!'

And that, surely, is the link that runs between *Samskara* and *Avasthe*: the hypocrisy of great men. In Ananthamurthy's debut, the ordinary brahmins of the agrahara are duplicitous and self-serving. But it is Praneshacharya, brahmin of brahmins, jewel of Kashi, abstemious philosopher, who must reckon with his spiralling attraction to an untouchable woman, indeed the sudden awakening of his libido. Much of the novel is spent in self-flagellation, yet even at the height of his fears about the loss of his brahminhood he does not consider the impact of this fulfilment upon the woman he has bedded, or the societal roles that have enabled it – he assumes he has elevated her by his touch. In *Avasthe*, Gowda's political hypocrisy is laid bare by a young firebrand still unspoiled by the compromises of electoral politics, most likely also the source of a series of articles in a Kannada tabloid that colour the choices in Krishnappa's life in the worst possible light. In this young man who is doing him so much damage Gowda sees a reflection of himself, and finds, perhaps, his redemption.

No one is spared Ananthamurthy's unswerving eye. One fascinating minor character – and this is a novel enlivened by such presences – is the silent hermit who lives in a cave up on a hill outside town: 'an old man with a long beard, naked except for a piece of cloth covering his crotch'. Krishnappa, still in college, trying to understand his political and social self, takes to visiting the hermit. They share tasteless meals, a nearby dog getting an equal share, and still the hermit is resolute in not speaking. He goes to town to sing verses from the Bhagavad Gita and lives on the rice, dal and fruit people drop into his bowl. Krishnappa cannot decide if he is an idiot or a savant. Yet even this egoless man is forgiven nothing. Years later, Krishnappa reads in the *Illustrated Weekly* that this hermit now enjoys the status of metamorph and godman, his thousands of devotees calling him Sarpasiddheshwarananda.

It is curious that Ananthamurthy barely notes the years of ascendancy, the triumphs that bring Krishnappa this popular reverence: the fasts, the battles against entrenched feudal forces, the victories on the legislative floor. Ananthamurthy seems to suggest something else about memory here. In our final reckoning – and isn't it scarier to have to do that here on earth, with ourselves, than in front of some ethereal judiciary – in our final reckoning, the mind does not revert to victory. When we each think back on our lives, this novel tells us, we will recall how we have loved and how we have failed.

Translator's Acknowledgements

I thank U.R. Ananthamurthy's family, Anuradha and Vivek Shanbhag in particular, for asking me to undertake this translation of *Avasthe,* and Esther Ananthamurthy for granting me the permission to publish the translation. With his personal involvement, Vivek has played a crucial role throughout the publication process. I owe him a special debt of gratitude. I am grateful also to Shruti Debi, proprietor of the Debi Agency, New Delhi, for her valuable editorial contribution. I am grateful to the National Endowment for the Arts, Washington, D.C., for awarding me the 2018 Literature Fellowship that enabled me to undertake this translation. Finally, I thank Rahul Soni of HarperCollins India for editing and facilitating the publication of my translation of *Avasthe.*

Narayan Hegde
Setauket, N.Y.
20 September 2020

About the Author and the Translator

U.R. Ananthamurthy (1932–2014) is one of India's greatest literary figures and public intellectuals. His publications include novels, short stories, poetry, translations and essays in literary and cultural criticism. He has been awarded the Padma Bhushan and the Jnanpith Award.

Narayan Hegde is an Emeritus Professor of English at the State University of New York, Old Westbury, USA. He is a recipient of the Katha Translation Award and the National Endowment for the Arts Fellowship for Literature. He is part of a team translating the fifteenth-century Kannada Mahabharata epic by Kumaravyasa, scheduled to be published by the Harvard University Press under the Murty Classical Library of India series.

HARPERPERENNIAL

Harper Perennial presents special editions of its finest books in translation

Apradhini
Shivani
Translated from the Hindi by Ira Pande

Avasthe
U.R. Ananthamurthy
Translated from the Kannada by Narayan Hegde

Blue Is Like Blue
Vinod Kumar Shukla
Translated from the Hindi by Arvind Krishna Mehrotra and Sara Rai

Diary of a Malayali Madman
N. Prabhakaran
Translated from the Malayalam by Jayasree Kalathil

Farewell, Mahatma
Devibharathi
Translated from the Tamil by N. Kalyan Raman

The Golden Gandhi Statue from America
Subimal Misra
Translated from the Bengali by V. Ramaswamy

A Name for Every Leaf
Ashok Vajpeyi
Translated from the Hindi by Rahul Soni

Moustache
S. Hareesh
Translated from the Malayalam by Jayasree Kalathil

Seven Sixes Are Forty-Three
Kiran Nagarkar
Translated from the Marathi by Shubha Slee

Shameless
Taslima Nasreen
Translated from the Bengali by Arunava Sinha

HARPERPERENNIAL

Age of Frenzy
Mahabaleshwar Sail
Translated from the Konkani by Vidya Pai

A Life Incomplete
Nanak Singh
Translated from the Punjabi by Navdeep Suri

Mohanaswamy
Vasudhendra
Translated from the Kannada by Rashmi Terdal

The Music of Solitude
Krishna Sobti
Translated from the Hindi by Vasudha Dalmia

No Presents Please
Jayant Kaikini
Translated from the Kannada by Tejaswini Niranjana

A Preface to Man
Subhash Chandran
Translated from the Malayalam by Fathima E.V.

The Secret Garland
Andal
Translated from the Tamil by Archana Venkatesan

Shala
Milind Bokil
Translated from the Marathi by Vikrant Pande

The Weary Generations
Abdullah Hussein
Translated from the Urdu by the author

Written in Tears
Arupa Patangia Kalita
Translated from the Assamese by Ranjita Biswas

HARPERPERENNIAL

Bhima
M.T. Vasudevan Nair
Translated from the Malayalam by Gita Krishnankutty

Chemmeen
Thakazhi Sivasankara Pillai
Translated from the Malayalam by Anita Nair

Ghachar Ghochar
Vivek Shanbhag
Translated from the Kannada by Srinath Perur

Hindutva or Hind Swaraj
U.R. Ananthamurthy
Translated from the Kannada by Keerti Ramachandra and Vivek Shanbhag

The Liberation of Sita
Volga
Translated from the Telugu by T. Vijay Kumar and C. Vijayasree

A Life Misspent
Suryakant Tripathi Nirala
Translated from the Hindi by Satti Khanna

The Sea Lies Ahead
Intizar Husain
Translated from the Urdu by Rakhshanda Jalil

Selected Poems
Joy Goswami
Translated from the Bengali by Sampurna Chattarji

Wild Animals Prohibited
Subimal Misra
Translated from the Bengali by V. Ramaswamy

Wild Words
Malathi Maithri, Salma, Kutti Revathi and Sukirtharani
Translated from the Tamil by Lakshmi Holmström

HarperCollins *Publishers* India

At HarperCollins India, we believe in telling the best stories and finding the widest readership for our books in every format possible. We started publishing in 1992; a great deal has changed since then, but what has remained constant is the passion with which our authors write their books, the love with which readers receive them, and the sheer joy and excitement that we as publishers feel in being a part of the publishing process.

Over the years, we've had the pleasure of publishing some of the finest writing from the subcontinent and around the world, including several award-winning titles and some of the biggest bestsellers in India's publishing history. But nothing has meant more to us than the fact that millions of people have read the books we published, and that somewhere, a book of ours might have made a difference.

As we look to the future, we go back to that one word— a word which has been a driving force for us all these years.

Read.

Harper Collins · 4th · HARPER PERENNIAL · HARPER BUSINESS · HARPER BLACK · हार्पर हिन्दी

HarperCollins *Children's Books* · HARPER DESIGN · HARPER VANTAGE · Harper Sport